THE KISSIMMEE KID

Buell steamed past it full charge and hurled himself at Cam. Evelyn watched Cam turn and kneel and open his arms.

Her own reunion with Cam was more dignified. She allowed only a solemn handshake. Cam said, "How in the world are you, girl?"

"Well," answered Evelyn, "we're here and I'm glad of it only I'm so hot I think I might be dead."

Cam said that he didn't mind the heat. "But why didn't you wait at the house for me? Didn't Lavaliere give you my message?"

Evelyn sniffed. "She didn't give us any message. She told us about Reba and the rustlers. She's peculiar. This whole place is peculiar. What's the matter with it?"

"There's nothing the matter with it," said Camfield. "It's part of the Kissimmee Prairie."

Also in paperback from Beech Tree Books

Patricia Beatty
Wait for Me, Watch for Me, Eula Bee

Patricia Clapp
Constance

Barbara Cohen
The Innkeeper's Daughter

Isabelle Holland
Now Is Not Too Late

Johanna Hurwitz
Tough-Luck Karen

Honoré Morrow
On to Oregon!

Vera and Bill Cleaver

THE KISSIMMEE KID

BEECH TREE BOOKS

New York

Printed in the United States of America

Library of Congress Cataloging in Publication Data

Cleaver, Vera. The Kissimmee Kid.
SUMMARY: To add to the confusion life has already
dealt her, 12-year-old Evelyn encounters some startling
contradictions when she and her younger brother visit
their sister and brother-in-law who live in Florida.
[1. Brothers and sisters — Fiction.   2. Florida —
Fiction]   I. Cleaver, Bill, joint author.   II. Title.
PZ7.C57926Ki [Fic] 80-29262 ISBN 0-688-10975-6

First Beech Tree edition, 1991
1   3   5   7   9   10   8   6   4   2

Authors' Note

The Kissimmee Prairie lands lie north of Lake Okeechobee in the state of Florida. The prairie is a reality. The town of Belle Plain is fictitious.

One

ONE CHOSEN DAY two citizens of a family named Chestnut went from their home which was located in an old comfortable town situated on the Gulf side of Florida's central coast. Their destination was a spot on the Kissimmee Prairie. The town nearest to this spot went by the name of Belle Plain.

Evelyn Chestnut was twelve years old and her brother Buell was nine. They traveled by bus and at every stop several passengers were discharged and were replaced by others.

Evelyn held her God box in her lap. A crafted gift from her brother-in-law Camfield, it usually served as a storehouse for her wishes and prayers, piles of them, all set to paper with care and much forethought, but now its important content was a cake decorated with glazed cherries and strongly flavored with imitation maple extract. This confection was the product of one of her many varying moods of which she was fond.

Fond was she too of her dreams and inward visions and her ability to take a dull fact and make such a remarkable thing of it that her listener or listeners would gasp. She liked her gloomy tales best, for she was a tall, strong child of abrasive personality. One who stood in front of her mirror for long periods, staring at her image, wondering if there might be another being hidden inside her visible self. Her mirror did not say.

Now sitting beside Buell in the southbound bus, she turned her head to avoid the sight of her reflection in the tinted, glare-proof window. Her appearance had never pleased her and didn't now.

The bus approached and crossed a bridge spanning a channel, and from their seats directly behind that of the driver's the two Chestnuts looked down into swift-flowing water weaving its way through cypress swamp.

"That was the Suwannee River," said Buell, standing to lean and rest his chin against the back of the driver's seat. "A man named Stephen Foster wrote a song about it. My dad's a music teacher and he told me that."

"You're a little mixed up on your geography," said the bus driver. "That was not the Suwannee River."

"You like music?"

"I can stand the old kind if it don't get too close to me," said the bus driver. "The new kind ought to be buried somewhere. All that whining and gagging."

Buell held a paper bag containing six pomander balls. "We're going to Major Peacock's ranch. It's near Belle Plain."

"I gotcha," said the bus driver. "I know exactly where it is."

"Going to stay till our mom and dad come back from St. Louis."

"And what are your mom and dad doing in St. Louis?"

"Our dad was born there and he wanted to look at it again. And he wanted Mama to have a vacation from Evvie and me. She works awful hard taking care of us all the time and gets tired. They took our little brother with them though. His name is Theo. Major Peacock's ranch has got cowboys."

"I should hope so," said the bus driver.

"Camfield is one. He's my brother-in-law. He married my oldest sister when I was seven and they lived in our garage till I got to be eight. Camfield used to be an art teacher. When he and Reba got married he was making a picture with pink birds in it. You ever seen a pink bird?"

"Flamingoes," said the bus driver. "They must have been flamingoes."

"Yes," agreed Buell, "they must have been. Cam's picture had a blue prince in it too. The prince was feeding the birds. But one night a mean boy crawled in the window at Cam's school and put big holes in his picture. So then Cam got mad and looked in the newspaper to see if he could find a different kind of a job and he found out that Major Peacock was looking for some cowboys and that's when he got to be one on the Major's ranch. See?"

"It's not a good idea for me to talk to the passengers while the bus is in motion," said the bus driver. "But before you go back to your seat you might as well tell me the rest of your tale. Who was the little darling who cut the holes in your brother-in-law's picture and why did he do it?"

Buell moved around to stand beside the driver, pushing his legs apart as far as they would go and swinging his paper bag. He knew how to flourish a story and told this one with the tolerance of an old man. "It was a boy named Wilson Padgett. He was in Camfield's class at school and everybody was scared of him. He hated Cam."

"Why?"

"It was because of values," answered Buell, losing a little ground. "You know what values are?"

"I know how much a pound of hamburger costs me every time I go to the grocery market," said the bus driver. "If that's a value then I sure know about it."

"Hamburger is not a value," said Buell. "That's something you buy and you only have to think about it for a minute. Values are what you think about when you read something or hear some music or see a picture somebody has painted. Stuff like that. Most people don't know about values and they don't care about them. They don't like to think. It hurts them. That's what Camfield told me and that's why he quit being a teacher. He couldn't teach people how to think and he was supposed to. So now he's a cowboy and doesn't have to worry about people thinking. All he has to worry about now is himself and Reba."

"I get the picture," said the bus driver. "Your brother-in-law is one of them arty fellas and Wilson Padgett isn't."

Buell deliberated. He left his position beside the bus driver's seat and from the aisle leaned in to put a whispered question to Evelyn. "Is Camfield arty?"

"Of course he is," snapped Evelyn. "You know he is. Why do you ask me such a fool question? Pull up your pants and leave your nose alone. You want it to grow sideways?"

Still whispering, Buell asked, "What about Wilson Padgett?"

"Wilson Padgett is a mistake," said Evelyn, making one of her insight judgments. "Somebody ought to take him down to Key West and push him off."

Buell went back to the bus driver. "Wilson Padgett is not arty. He's a mistake. Camfield's arty. You can't tell he's different from anybody else unless he wants you to, though. He's strong. When we had to move from our old house to our new one and Dad couldn't get anybody to come after his piano, Cam got some guys to help him get it as far as the street, but then they ran off so Cam pushed it by himself down to our new house. Mama wouldn't look. Reba either. But I did."

Said the bus driver, "Did you say Reba is your oldest sister? The one married to Cam?"

"She's twenty now," said Buell. "When she got

13

married to Camfield she was eighteen. She didn't want to go to college. She wanted to get married. You ever seen a pomander ball?"

"If that's one of those values you were telling me about, I reckon I haven't," replied the bus driver. "Your grandpa asked me to let you off in front of the Peacock ranch. It's on this side of Belle Plain and we'll be there in about fifteen minutes so you'd better start getting your things together."

Buell knelt and opened his paper bag and tenderly withdrew an orange so heavily studded with whole, embedded cloves that none of its thick skin was visible. Attached to it was a long loop of shimmering ribbon. With a shiny smile Buell offered this perfumed gift. "This here's a pomander ball. Cam taught me how to make them. He's got one his mother made for him when he was a baby and he's twenty-five now. You take this one home to your wife and tell her to hang it up in her closet. It won't ever rot. It'll make everything smell good. I really like you."

"I like you too," said the bus driver and hung the pomander ball around his neck.

It was June and far out on the ranges of Major Peacock's empire black cattle and red cattle stood in the hot wind, stood among the tinted bunchgrasses and under the sequestered trees. The air was yellow and to Evelyn, who had never had much of a bent for scenery or the temptation to wonder about it, all of this stillness and distance appeared as some lost wisdom, like a history lesson about the ancients.

The bus came to a stop in front of the ranch's admitting gate. It was closed, but just inside it there waited a young woman. She was sloe-eyed and long-limbed, an embrowned and indolent little prairie flower in ankle boots and a red, short-skirted dress. For the departing bus driver she had a blown kiss and to Evelyn and Buell she said, "Hey. I'm Lavaliere. Did you have a nice trip?"

"It wasn't anything extra," said Evelyn.

"Are you wondering am I the Major's daughter?" said Lavaliere. "Everybody does."

"I was looking at your legs," said Evelyn. "What makes them shine like that?"

"I oil them," said Lavaliere. "I work for the Major and he likes everything oiled so it'll work faster. Camfield asked me to come down here and meet you. He's out riding fence and couldn't come himself. Just let me get this gate locked up again and then I'll take you to his house. It's a piece from here, but if you won't melt before we get there I won't either."

"Why couldn't Reba have come to meet us?" asked Evelyn. Inside the flat, rubber-soled shoes she wore every day, year round, her feet itched. She watched Lavaliere lock the gate and turn to take Buell's suitcase from him.

"All those cows," said Buell. "Cam never said

there were so many." He was awed and raptly excited and curious about all. "Where are the cowboys? Where's the Major?"

"It's payday," explained Lavaliere, "so most of the cow hunters have mooched off to town and the Major is home shampooing his eye."

"He's what?" said Evelyn.

"The Major has a glass eye," said Lavaliere. "And he says he likes to wash it every Saturday. I've never seen him do it. I don't know a thing about glass eyes, but that's what he says. Let's go this way."

"I sure would like to see the Major's house," said Buell. "I sure would. Maybe he's sitting on his front porch and we could just kind of walk past it and say hey. I brought him a pomander ball. I'll bet he'd like to have it now."

"Little dear," said Lavaliere, "the Major's house is way back in there and he never sits on his front porch because he doesn't like porches. The only things he likes are his cows and dogs. And what he chucks into his stomach. He loves to eat."

"Well," commented Evelyn, "Reba is a good cook." The rich and wonderful disorder through which they passed now, its high-sprung ferns, hangings of gray Spanish moss, its elvin flowers, all of these graces were food for a long view, yet to Evelyn they were merely countrified jottings. She watched the swing of Lavaliere's skirt. "I asked you a minute ago why Reba didn't come to meet us and you didn't answer."

Without turning, Lavaliere said, "Reba is in town

working for Mr. Jim at The Orange Blossom Cafe and she's doing all right for herself too. She told me she's making three times the money the Major was paying her. Mr. Jim doesn't stay open on Sundays so on Saturday nights Cam goes after her and then takes her back on Sunday evening. She rents a room in town, shares it with Mr. Jim's cashier. It doesn't cost much. Didn't you know all this?"

"We didn't know of any of it," said Evelyn. "Reba doesn't like to write letters and the only time she phones is when it's somebody's birthday or something like that. When Dad and Mama decided to go to St. Louis they called her and asked her if we could come here for a little vacation of our own, and she said we could if we could entertain ourselves. But she didn't tell us she wasn't working for Major Peacock any more. I think that's peculiar. She's a married woman and married women are supposed to come home every night. Why doesn't she? What happened?"

"Dear," said Lavaliere, "I don't know all the trifles concerning Cam and Reba and the Major and the troubles that have caused things to be the way they are. Reba didn't like living out here and she hated every day she worked for the Major, and she wants Cam to quit too only he keeps putting her off. I don't know why she only comes home to be with Cam on Saturday nights and Sundays, except maybe she figures if she sticks it out long enough Cam will give in quicker. Cam gets along with the Major but Reba never did. The day she went off to town to work for

Mr. Jim she and the Major had an awful fuss. As soon as she left he came sweating and wheezing down to my house and said for me to come cook for him till Reba got over her mad. I told him I didn't know how to cook, not like Reba, and he said how would I like to take my daddy and both of us go and live under a tree, but not one of his, you understand."

"Your daddy," said Evelyn and looked around as if she might see that person dangling from a bush.

"So now," said Lavaliere, "I cook for the Major and keep his house. Daddy and I live in one of his cabins. The Major says I can't fry water without burning it, but he can't get anybody else to come out here and do for him. It's too lonesome. He's dying to get Reba back, but even if he asked her she wouldn't come. She doesn't like him, she doesn't like the way he treats people, and she doesn't like his dogs."

"Dogs don't hurt anything," said Evelyn. "I think all of this is very peculiar. My dad would about have a stew if he knew Reba was working in a cafe. She doesn't know how to do anything but cook because when she was in high school she wasn't studying books. She was studying Camfield. But she's not common."

"Neither is The Orange Blossom Cafe," said Lavaliere. "It's a nice place with white tablecloths and all. And Mr. Jim is a nice Greek man. He doesn't allow anybody to spit on the floor or anything like that."

Buell, who had been lagging silently, decided to come to life. "How much farther is it, Lavaliere?"

"It's just there," replied Lavaliere, pointing. "Look. See it?"

"Yes, I see it!" screamed Buell. His eyes couldn't take it all in fast enough.

They had left that first vital forest behind them and crossed a treeless area where white sugar sands supported stiff palmetto and wire grasses, where the sun's glare created trembling air-images, and there were no sounds save the rattling of fronds. But now spread out before them was a great living floor populated by pines and oaks and a wilderness dwelling that to Evelyn's eyes looked as if it had been teased up out of the earth. She had expected something kinder and bigger, a red farmhouse with a chimney and shutters or a white cottage surrounded by a hedge of roses, but there it sat, brown and glum and little. There was a pickup truck parked at one of its sides and at its naked front there stretched a dirt road curving out to the main, black-topped road. Metal boundary fence enclosed all of this, running in both directions, sinking from sight where the land dipped but then rising again on the higher, faraway grounds.

Buell, incapable of disappointment or fatigue, said, "Oh, it's cute," and charged away through the trees waving his arms and shrieking.

Evelyn stood motionless. The silence was dreary. It filled her ears and her head. "That's where Cam and Reba live? That's their house?"

Lavaliere set Buell's suitcase on the ground. "That's it. Cam's not home yet. If he was you'd see that old marshtackie he always rides wandering around."

"What," asked Evelyn, "is a marshtackie?"

"It's a cow pony," answered Lavaliere. And said, "Cam should be home soon. I have to go back now. You can manage your suitcases the rest of the way, can't you?"

"Awful," said Evelyn, unable to feel even a drop of sympathy. "I have never been in such an ugly place. I know I have never seen such an ugly house. What's it stuck way out here for?"

"Dear," said Lavaliere, "this is a ranch and it's big."

"I see it," said Evelyn. "Don't you think I see it? But that house. Look at it. Is that a house? Looks like a trash heap to me. No wonder Reba doesn't want to live in it. I don't blame her."

"It's not just for somebody to live in," said Lavaliere. "Mainly it's to scare off the rustlers."

"Is that so," said Evelyn.

"So they won't come," said Lavaliere. "You know what rustlers are, don't you?"

"I might have heard about them," hedged Evelyn. "Right off it doesn't come to my mind exactly what they are. I'm thinking we shouldn't have come. Maybe we won't stay. Maybe tomorrow we'll go back home. Our grandfather and grandmother will let us stay with them till Dad and Mama and Theo get back from St. Louis."

"Rustlers are cattle thieves," said Lavaliere. "Don't

you watch television or go to the picture shows?"

"We aren't allowed," said Evelyn. "Unless it's about ballet or has music. Stuff like that. Movies and television don't interest me fortunately."

Lavaliere fluffed her hair and incuriously asked, "What does?"

"I like to ride my bicycle and sleep," answered Evelyn. "Does the bus come past here every day?"

"I suppose it does," said Lavaliere. "I never watch for it because I almost never go anyplace. There's a phone in Cam's house. You could call the bus station and find out. Listen, I have to go now but probably I'll see you this evening if you go to town with Cam. On paydays he always stops by the Major's house at suppertime. I'll fix it so you can see him feed his dogs. It'll be something you can talk about when you go home."

"I've already got plenty to talk about," returned Evelyn. Disappointed, annoyed, she hefted both suitcases and started out across the meadow toward the house. Buell was already at its door, pounding on it and screaming his arrival.

Evelyn watched him pull the door open and disappear. Buell could play "Light Is Your Bark, Brothers, Rest on Your Oars" on the piano without missing a note. He had their father's eager readiness for living and their mother's sweet patience, whereas she, Evelyn, was possessed of so little of both of these properties that she wondered at times if she actually, truly, was a Chestnut. She had never felt fully related to either her father or mother. All of that energy of theirs, their quick laughter, their talented hands and feet. The baby Theo hadn't settled them down. They still danced together whenever the notion hit them.

They were good to her, her parents were. In those times when she had lain sick, sniveling with a cold or suffering one of her other unattractive woes, they had always come, clucking their concerns, offering their faultless sympathies. Yet the minute her health returned so did their ways of looking at her and talking with her, as if they saw and heard in her something strangely afloat, a breakdown of some kind. Once her father had tried to teach her how to play the piano, but after a dozen or so lessons she had been gently pardoned and released.

After the piano lessons she had tackled a study of herself, shrewdly soliciting the opinions of Velda Grace Renfroe. Velda Grace had groped her way through this job for she had never met a new idea. She herself had no followers. Her father owned a mattress factory and at school she clung to Evelyn as if Evelyn might be her last hope. Like Evelyn, she could make a compliment last a month.

Toward the little gaunt wilderness house Evelyn plodded. To the west where the wild turf arched and then leveled off there had appeared a figure on a horse. It moved toward a cluster of black cows and stopped. The cows closed around it, hiding it from Evelyn's vision. She gazed upon this scene without thought. The bigger of the two suitcases was heavy. She accepted the burden of them as she accepted the practical beating of her heart and the rhythm of her lungs. Her God box gouged the soft fleshy part of her forearm.

When she reached the back step of the house she slung both suitcases up onto the wooden stoop and stood beside it holding on to the box. After a minute of this she went up onto the stoop herself and sat down beside the bigger case. In a loud voice she said, "Buell, you can come out of there and get your suitcase now. I've carried it this far and I'm no elephant. I didn't take you to raise. This is as much my vacation as it is yours. Buell!"

"You don't have to yell at me like that," said Buell from just inside the screened door. He pushed it open and came out onto the stoop and crouched beside her, offering a jar of water with ice cubes in it. "They got a refrigerator."

"What of it," said Evelyn. She drank from the jar until it was nearly empty and then poured what remained over her head.

Shivering with excitement yet holding himself in check, Buell watched this performance. "Cam's not home."

"No," said Evelyn "he's out there."

Buell jumped up. "Where? I don't see him."

"You have to look hard. Look way out there where those cows are."

"Yes!" cried Buell. "I can see them! But I don't see Cam. Are you sure he's with the cows?"

"I'm sure."

"What's he doing with them?"

"How would I know? Take your suitcase inside and put it somewhere. When you come back out bring me some more water. I'm parched and need to rest. That Lavaliere. She's ridiculous. I'll bet that's not even her real name. You remember that gold thing Grandma Chestnut wears around her neck when she comes to see us and is all dressed up? That thing on a chain? That's a lavaliere. It isn't anybody's name."

"Let's go find Cam," said Buell.

"Let's not," said Evelyn. "I've chased after you all I'm going to this day."

Buell grinned. He knew better.

So presently they left the sketchy comfort of the stoop and again set out across the sun-smitten grassland, Buell running on ahead and Evelyn, still hugging her God box, following.

There was the monotony of broomsedge. Tall and reddish brown, it moved with the wind. There was vine and there was bush smothered in vine. There was white bloom and pink and the seeking wild bees rose droning from the meadow pockets.

None of this caught at Evelyn's mind. She had no thirst for it. She kept her eyes on the knot of cows and, as the distance between it and her lessened, she saw Cam moving around, on foot now, among the animals. One by one they bounded away to the green gloom of the trees. The sky was bare and pale. Along the fence line the marshtackie grazed. It might have been painted there for all the notice Buell gave it. He steamed past it full charge and hurled himself at Cam. Evelyn watched Cam turn and kneel and open his arms.

Her own reunion with Cam was more dignified. She allowed only a solemn handshake. Cam said, "How in the world are you, girl?"

"Well," answered Evelyn, "we're here and I'm glad of it only I'm so hot I think I might be dead."

Cam said that he didn't mind the heat. "But why didn't you wait at the house for me? Didn't Lavaliere give you my message?"

Evelyn sniffed. "She didn't give us any message. She told us about Reba and the rustlers. She's peculiar. This whole place is peculiar. What's the matter with it?"

"There's nothing the matter with it," said Camfield. "It's part of the Kissimmee Prairie."

"I see you've still got the ganglies," said Evelyn. "You'd get rid of them if you'd eat like I do. I eat everything even if I don't like it."

"You've got a cute horse!" roared Buell. "Let me try on your hat. No, it's too big for me. You can have it back. What time are we going to town to get Reba? I want to see the Major. I'm going to give him one of my pomander balls. Why did the cows run away? I want to see them." He twisted from Cam's grasp and quick as a snail darter sped out across the fields toward the trees.

"Buell!" shouted Cam. "Come back here!"

"Oh, let him go," said Evelyn. "He won't get too

close to the cows. He only wants to look. Are you sure all this out here is what you call prairie? I thought prairie only grew out in Kansas or somewhere like that."

Cam had that kind of face seen on marble pedestals in museums. It had long sad lines and in his eyes where once there had shone the gleam of a high, rebellious heart there was now only a kind of loose pleasantness. Once he had fought and fought hard for those things in which he had believed, the marvels of the student mind, the worth of knowledge, the belief in humankind's ties with nature, histories, and sciences. But Camfield had lost his fight. To machines and numbers and crowding and the demand for speed in what he taught and how he taught it he had lost, and now, like those who had defeated him, he asked only to be allowed to go his own simple way.

Answering Evelyn's question, he said, "Evvie, prairie is only a word for a certain type of land. What you see here is a part of the Kissimmee Prairie."

"Well, fiddle," said Evelyn. "I wish somebody had told me that before now. It's embarrassing not to know things like that." She looked down at her God box. "I brought you a cake. I made it myself so probably it's not very good. It tasted all right raw but if you don't like it you can throw it out. It's in here. We didn't have a regular cake box so I brought it in here."

"Old lady," said Cam, taking the box from her. "If you made it I'll like it." He passed his hand over the box's grimy cover.

26

"I guess I should have washed it," said Evelyn. "But I don't have time to do all the stuff I'm supposed to do. In a family like ours it's always something. A couple of weeks ago Theo was sicker than sin and Mama had to carry him to our doctor. It was only a little old bitty fever like all babies get all the time but the way everybody went on you'd have thought it was a heart attack. Mama kept me home from school for three days because Theo wouldn't let anybody else hold him. When he's sick he never does." This story was a lie. The truth was, in illness or health her very presence was cause for Theo to beat on anything handy with his spoon or his fists and make alarmed noises. He had another little trick which he used to torment and disgust her. He would store food in one of his cheeks like a squirrel and then when she went to him, to lift him, to try and cuddle him, he would collect the soggy mess in his mouth with his tongue, lean and spit it on her. Theo was an expert food spitter but was not careless with this power. It was only for her, for Evelyn.

Finished with her lie, Evelyn turned and looked toward the trees. Between their boles there was light like at early dusk and there were the nibbling cows. The wind was at their backs and they were all turned in the same direction, moving across a tilt in the land to where bands of pines and oaks gave way to plain.

Half-drugged with the dreamlike quality of this scene, Evelyn said, "I guess we'd better go find Buell. He never thinks somebody else might want to do something different from what he wants. What about your horse? Will he run away?"

"His name is Spirit," said Cam. "No, he won't run away. He knows it's payday and about my quitting time. I told him. You've heard of horse sense? Well, Spirit has quite a bit of it. We understand each other. His ancestors were of early Spanish stock and you don't see much of his kind around anymore. Most Florida cowboys prefer bigger mounts like those on western ranges, but I like Spirit. He's quick and smart. He'll go on home."

Walking beside her through the grass sea that weaved, that rippled with each wash of the wind, he stopped twice and Evelyn was obliged to stop with him and squat and examine little runes of prairie life, an empty nest skillfully molded and now abandoned, a web strung between two stalks, the shell of a tree snail. As if they were a part of his very substance, as if they held for him some lost promise, as if he loved them, Cam bent his face to these things and Evelyn, watching, made a bleak and harsh statement, saying, "I knew it. I knew you weren't finished with that. I knew you didn't want to come down here and be a cowboy. So why'd you run away? Reba was on your side and so was I. And Mama and Dad. I'm so mad at the whole mess. I'm so mad at people."

"Don't be," said Camfield. "Things here aren't so bad. This is an experience for both Reba and me. We're not unhappy. We're both working and we're saving our money. I have plans."

"You have plans? What plans? Does Reba know about them?"

"Plans. For a better life for us. And no, Reba doesn't know about them. I'll tell her when the time comes."

"And when is that going to be?"

"Soon," answered Camfield. Some far-apart clouds had appeared on the far horizon and Cam stood. In his palm he still held the snail shell, but after they had gone a few steps he tossed it away.

Under a tree in the still and shadowed forest they found Buell standing beside a rabbit. The animal was mangled and dead. There was blood on its face and what was left of its body, and it lay on its side with its paws stiff.

Whispering his horror and disbelief, Buell said, "It's dead. What killed it?"

"Son," said Camfield, "I don't know what did it. There are lots of bigger animals out here and rabbits are fair game for them, that's all I can tell you."

"I don't want it dead," said Buell, outraged. He bounded to Evelyn and gave her shirttail a yank. "I said I don't want it dead! Didn't you hear me?"

She slapped his hand away. "Be quiet. It's only a rabbit and he's dead and we can't bring him back, so hush. If you don't I'm going to put my hand down my throat and turn myself inside out and then you'll have something to scream about sure enough."

Cam was beside the animal, pulling clumps of grass from the earth, digging into it with his hands, creating a quick little grave. The leaves of the tree rustled and Buell and Evelyn watched.

At the last moment, as Cam lowered the remains of the rabbit into the hole and pushed the dirt and grass back into place, Buell sprang forward, crying, "Wait! Wait! We forgot to tell him we loved him! We forgot to tell him we were sorry!"

Cam rose and extended his hand. "Buell, it's all right. He knew. Come away now. Come with Evvie and me."

"He didn't know," shrieked Buell. "How could he know if we didn't tell him?"

At the back of her head Evelyn's brain pushed and swelled and floundered. She hated the dead rabbit, hated the way the scene sucked at her. Most of all in this moment she hated all of those people back home, all of those walking around in their big bossy bodies carrying their little petty concerns. If it were not for them Camfield and Reba would not be in this crazy place and neither would she. She would be in St. Louis with her parents or with her grandparents, in one of their air-conditioned bedrooms, sleeping, having herself a good dream, drowsing through it, discarding the unpleasant parts, entertaining the pleasant ones. Those who populated those half-awake dreams of hers came to the auditorium where she performed on the piano so brilliantly that the crystal in the chandeliers splintered and fell. They fought to kiss the hem of her gown and spoke of her great beauty the way grown-ups speak at prayer.

But all of that was far away now. Here there were no dreams and no place to go privately to create one. There was only realness.

The light, leaking down through the overhead leafage, was changing, deepening, and Cam, in charge of himself and in charge of Buell, was looking at her and saying, "Old lady? Old lady, where are you? Aren't you coming with us?"

"Oh, of course I am," said Evelyn. "I am certainly not going to spend the night out here by myself so of course I'm coming with you. But not right this minute. You all go ahead on and I'll catch up with you."

Cam hesitated. "Are you sure?"

"Sure," said Evelyn and like a dog shook herself. Her eyes grew hard. Tomorrow, she thought, Buell and I are going to get back on that bus and go home. We shouldn't have come. And Cam and Reba don't belong here either. Look at Cam, bucket of bones.

Hand in hand, Cam and Buell were going away from her and in a straggle the cows were coming back through the trees. Cam had forgotten the God box and she lifted it and sniffed a dirty tear.

She sat on the ground and said, "Well, fiddle," and looked at her feet. And looked up and saw her bird, a live duplicate of the one on the cover of her God box. Bright of plumage, scarlet-bright, he flashed from bough to bough and peered out at her like some little puffed-up priest, and his sweet notes, wistfully inquiring, tenderly sympathizing, touched something dead and distant in her. So sudden was this and so searing, so depthful, that the breath in her stopped. Afraid to move, afraid to breathe, she stared at the bird. There was a moment of silence, but then again came an outpouring of song. The song was for her. The bird knew her. How could that be?

Wonderingly, Evelyn dared to lean forward. Enchanted, she wanted the enchanter's song to go on forever. There was a commotion taking place inside her. It had fingers and plucked at her old mechanical strings, freeing them. Something splashed. She closed her eyes.

When she opened her eyes she saw that the bird had gone backward on his branch, and was now observing her. He was standing under a wisp of Spanish moss being wafted back and forth, and as she watched, it dropped, settling on the songster's head like a little silver chaplet. "Oh!" she exclaimed. "Ohhhhh!" And the bird soared upward and was gone.

As in some fluid dream Evelyn stood, and after a moment of looking at the spot in the tree where the bird had been, left the forest on a run, calling out to Cam and Buell, calling, "Wait! Wait for me! I want to tell you about the bird I just saw! Wait!"

They didn't hear her. They were too far along, the little figure and the big one, tramping homeward, cutting their own trail.

And now the prairie, so alien to her before and cruel, lay charmed. Its molten colors and its sun and

wind turned her giddy. Its grass heads, wistful little spies, flowed with the wind, lisping, *You, you*. And, pale and altered, Evelyn stopped and stood in an attitude of listening. Like the bird, the grasses knew her and in an agony of remorse and self-discovery she looked down at them and then knelt among them. *You, you*, they chanted and she put her face down to them but was unable to formulate an answer.

Two

IT WAS NOT YET TIME for duskfall when Cam and the two Chestnuts left the outpost house, riding away from it in the pickup which shrieked and spit and jerked and otherwise complained until Cam set its wheels on a narrow sand road twisting back up into open rangeland, running on and on past open-air sheds and pole-type barns, past watering troughs and erect, free-standing silos.

The heat of the day was lifting and now to Evelyn's eyes the prairie, so strong and silent, looked fugitive. For a reason indistinct even to herself she had decided to save her secret, the one concerning the little scarlet priest-bird who had sung to her so confidingly. It made her feel wise and pure and forgiving, though she couldn't think what in her life there was that might need her forgiveness other than the fancied stories she told and they harmed no one. For her meeting with the Major and then the trip into Belle Plain she had mopped her face from chin to hairline with a damp washcloth and squirted her underarms with some of Reba's deodorant. She intended to impress the Major and discuss important things with him if that was his pleasure. She hoped he would not bring details of his past military life into their conversation, for she knew nothing about where wars were fought

or why. She had met only one real live soldier, an uncle to Velda Grace Renfroe. He was sixty years old and to see him salute the flag flying from its mast in front of the post office was a tingling sight.

Buell was ravenous to see Major Peacock. In his eagerness he almost fell from the truck when Cam pulled into a clearing and stopped before a flat-topped cabin. Its bare yard had been broom swept and on its porch there sat an old, bent man. He appeared to be asleep, yet every second or so, without opening his eyes, he would give his rocker a little push to set it in motion again.

Clutching his sack of pomander balls, Buell raced around the truck, stopped, peered and came running back to Evelyn. "It's him. It's the Major and he looks just like I knew he would, except I thought he'd be wearing his sword. What should I call him and am I supposed to salute?"

"That is not the Major," said Evelyn, alighting from the truck. "So you don't have to salute him and you can call him Mr. Workman because that's his name. He's Lavaliere's father and this is his house. Weren't you listening when Cam said we had to stop here first and visit a little with Mr. Workman?"

"He's asleep," said Buell in a tone of hopeful defeat. "So maybe we won't have to stay but just a minute."

They were required to sit on the cabin's steps for the better part of an hour while Mr. Workman, who preferred to be addressed by his first name, which was

Henry, talked. In the ways of conversation he was skilled once he got rolling. He had three tufts of white hair, one over each ear and one sticking up out of his frontal skull. His right hand was missing, but if ever he had grieved its loss he wasn't now. It had been a willing sacrifice made for a friend and he'd make it again if he had to. To Evelyn and Buell he displayed the stump. "It don't pain me anymore. You want to hear how it happened?"

"When I die I'm going to give all my organs to people who are still alive," said Evelyn. The thought was a new one and shocking and contained not an ounce of truthful intention. It would be all right if, when she died, they cut a lock of hair from her head, but other than that she was going to be buried whole.

"When I die they can give one of my hands to somebody if they need it," said Buell. "But I'm going to keep them both for myself while I'm still alive. Unless my dad or mother or somebody else in my family needs them worse than I do."

"Henry," said Cam, "before you get going on your faithful friend story maybe we'd better take a reading on what all you need from town this time."

"Aspirin," said Henry.

"You want the nourishing kind or just plain?" asked Cam.

"And go by the repair shop and see if my shoes are ready," said Henry. "I don't know what I did with the claim stub but you won't need it. Nick knows you and he knows my shoes. Oh, and get Lavaliere a little something or another, maybe a bar of that fancy pink soap like you got her before. You'll have to shell out for me temporarily. Right now I hadn't got a dollar on me."

"Aspirin, soap and shoes," said Camfield. "I'll bet your kitchen feels about as useful as a third leg."

"My kitchen isn't suffering any from loneliness," returned Henry. "I eat my breakfast in it every morning and Lavaliere and me eat our supper in it every night. This evening when she comes from the Major's house she's going to bring me blackberry cobbler and steak and tomorrow evening it'll be chicken. The Major don't like the dark meat and it's my favorite, so that's what I always eat."

Cam set his back against one of the porch posts. A gentleman in rough cowboy clothes, he pushed his hat back and lent his eyes and ears to the sundown prairie. "Go ahead, Henry. Tell the kids how you lost your hand."

"I shot it off myself," said Henry. He put his bare feet flat on the floor and, as if to impart some great and pious secret, bent forward. "I say I shot it off myself. Now one of you ask me why."

A muscle in Evelyn's thigh twitched and she said, "Well, it had to have been for something desperate." Some of Henry's upper teeth were missing, his body was too little for his clothes and there was something in the stamp of him, in his childlike eyes, that made her think of Velda Grace Renfroe. "It had to have been for something serious and awful, something queer," she said.

"Yes," agreed Buell in a wrinkled voice. "Something serious and awful and queer. But what?"

Plainly Henry was famished to tell his story. He drew himself erect in his chair and inclined his head and, as if it might be something precious to him, spoke his yarn with care and affection. "Have you," he inquired, "seen the Major's lake yet?"

"The Major owns a lake?" asked Evelyn. In her estimation Major Peacock shot up yet another notch. She pictured him standing in the lake's flashing center. He wore a bearskin cape and a chieftan's feathered headdress. His discoverer's sword, held aloft, gleamed. Behind him his uniformed regiment stood at stiff attention while an aide planted a flag.

"There was two gators lived in it," said Henry. "The Major named them Big Smith and Suzy and every day or so him and me would ride down to the lake and see could we spot them. The Major liked to feed them and always took them something to eat. Always took along a little pig and some firecrackers too. Big Smith didn't like it when the Major would pull the little pig's tail to make it squeal. He'd get real excited and that was part of the Major's fun. Big Smith didn't like the popping of the firecrackers either but he got so he'd swim right up and wait for the Major to throw him his handout. Suzy was a different breed. She wasn't very long in the up-and-at-'em department and would run off and hide when she'd see us. She had a big yellow belly on her and you could just see the hate in them big, bulgy eyes of hers."

"There was a man who came to our school and told us about alligators," said Evelyn. "If you feed them they get like those bears you see in parks. Dangerous. Everybody knows you aren't supposed to feed those bears you see in big parks and alligators are the same. You're supposed to leave alligators alone. I wouldn't feed one for a million bucks."

Crouched at Henry's knee, Buell said, "I want to hear the story. Let him tell it, Evvie."

"Not for two million bucks," said Evelyn.

Henry was rocking. "Well, the day I lost my hand it wasn't any different than any other. I remember I had Big Smith's lunch with me but I don't recall what it was."

"It was a mudfish," reminded Camfield.

"Sir?" said Henry.

"You've always told me it was a mudfish," said Cam.

"It was a mudfish," said Henry, as if he had remembered this dazzling detail himself. "And as soon as Big Smith had gobbled it down and saw there wasn't any more he turned around and started to go back out in the lake, but just then the Major pulled the little pig's tail. I guess he gave it a extra hard jerk, for the little porker let out a squeal and jumped. He went past me like he'd been shot out of a cannon. The Major jumped too. He didn't mean to and made a grab for me to check hisself but missed, and then there was the pig and Big Smith and the Major, all three in the water, and me standing there on the bank holding my gun. I should have killed Big Smith right then, but you know how you get rattled in a situation like that?"

"The Major shouldn't have pulled the pig's tail," said Evelyn. "That was mean."

"Let him tell his story," screamed Buell. "Everything I want to hear, you always mess it up."

"You're supposed to leave bears and birds alone too," said Evelyn. "You're not supposed to tease them and scare them and you're not supposed to kill them just so you can wear their hides and feathers just to make you look good when you discover a lake."

"What?" asked Henry. "Little lady, what did you say?"

"That's the way she talks," cried Buell. "Nobody ever knows what she means." He jerked his bag open, brought forth one of his pomander balls and laid it on Henry's lap. "Here. This is for you. I made it myself. Would you rather have one with some other color ribbon?"

"No," said Henry. "I like purple." He looked at the ball of artcraft as if it might be a moon someone had dropped on him.

"What about Big Smith and the Major?" said Evelyn. "And the pig. All three were in the water. That's where you left off."

Into Henry's face, his servile face, there crept the

humble vanity of his servile tale. On it his voice feasted. "The pig got away. I didn't see how it did, because my mind was too busy trying to decide what to do. I saw Big Smith going for the Major and the Major was trying to get away, but he couldn't. He had on heavy boots and the lake was kicking up a fuss because it was fixing to rain and with them two things against him he wasn't no match for Big Smith. Big Smith brought that big tail of his around and whopped the Major with it. Took his eye out and took his ear off and laid the Major's face open. Then he got the Major's foot in his jaws and tried to drag him under. He was going to drown him and would have if it hadn't been for me. By that time I was in the water too, and I grabbed the Major by the foot and commenced trying to pull him away from Big Smith. That only made Big Smith madder. So he let go of the Major and came after me. He clomped his jaw on my hand and wouldn't let go. To get it loose I had to shoot it off. My bullet got Big Smith too and I can tell you he was one surprised old bull. Now," said Henry, fixing Buell and Evelyn with a certain eye, "tell me what you think of that."

Buell sat back on his heels and released his breath. He made a comradely and emphatic declaration. "You had to do it. You had to. So you did and that's all."

"You must think a lot of the Major," said Evelyn, snatching at a thread of thought, "to do a thing like that for him."

"He's my friend," said Henry, bestowing upon

41

her a fierce, vulture's scrutiny. "Had it been my leg I would have done the same thing. I would have shot it off to save the Major. They don't come like him except about as often as it snows in August. He takened Lavaliere and me in when we didn't have any place else to go. Didn't ask too many questions either. Just said was I a cattleman and where was my wife and why did I leave my last job, and I told him my wife passed on when Lavaliere was twelve and cows was the only thing I knew and the reason I left my last job was because my boss cut back on his payroll and let me out."

Four cows had come up into the road running past Henry's cabin and he left his chair to cross the porch and stand on its top step, watching the animals bed down in the dirt. "The Major still thinks his inventory figure was some short last time," he said to Cam. "Wonder if those four was counted."

"Henry," said Cam in the easy manner of one exchanging a pleasantry, "this is June and the last inventory that I know anything about was taken six months ago. Don't tell me you're still trying to track down the Major's January shortages."

"He worries," fretted Henry. "And he hadn't got anybody to help him do that except me. And you. The others don't care. All they care about is payday. Did you know Tim Barnett quit this morning?"

"Yesterday when I was helping with the calf vaccinating he told me he was going to," commented Cam. Thinker without desk, artist without easel, teacher without pupil; there was a wind of health and confidence about him. On the western skyline the day was turning toward evening.

"He was a good cattle manager," said Henry, "but his personality was against him. He was always at sixes and sevens with the men and the Major too. You know, when you work for somebody you work for him, you don't chase around all over creation trying to change his ideas to suit yours every five minutes. What if everybody did that?"

"Henry," said Cam, "I'm just a cow man. That's all I was hired to be and that's all I am. I don't know about ideas. They used to be important to me but I've found I can live without them."

"It was Tim's own notion to go over to the university to study that course he took in beef cattle," said Henry. "It was to his benefit as much as it was to the Major's. The Major didn't force him to do it, so why did he think the Major should ought to pay him for the time it took him to take it?"

Cam shrugged. "I heard Tim and the Major had an agreement and when it came time to pay for it the Major backed down, but since it didn't concern me I didn't pay much attention to the talk. I liked Tim and I'm sorry he's gone but my loyalty is to the Major."

"He's not a happy person," said Henry pensively. "The men ought to take that into consideration but they don't." Confirmed in this view and prideful of his own standing with the Major, Henry went down the steps and walked toward the cows lying in the road, officially circling them, going around them twice, scrutinizing their rump brands and tattooed ear markings before returning to the chair on the porch.

Now the dusk was coming. Thin and brown, it swam through and over the trees and Cam said it was time to get on to the Major's house. At the last minute Buell ran back and left yet another of his pomander balls with Henry. "This one's for Lavaliere," he said, beaming his generosity and goodwill.

For Evelyn the ride to the Major's house was a sufferance. The time spent on Henry's porch had shortened and fatigued her enthusiasm for the coming meeting with Major Peacock. She had formed a dislike for him and in this Henry figured. Silly, groveling old drudge, so pitiable and maddeningly humble, so like Velda Grace Renfroe.

Buell had insisted on sitting next to the window on the passenger's side in the pickup and, in the fashion of a joy-riding dog, pushed his head out of the window as far as it would go. The wind made his eyes water and dragged his hair straight back.

The headlights to the truck were on and as they passed through the pasturelands Cam stopped several times, all three alighted and Cam used his high-powered flashlight to point out places of interest. Buell had to know the names of everything and their uses had to be explained to him.

There were tall, roofed, open-sided boxes designed to make available to cows and calves at all times salts and minerals so necessary to their health. There was a shed mounted on skids and enclosed within a fence wired to metal corner stakes. Nearby, just outside the fence, there was a water tank and there were water troughs and trees. Cam said the shed was a creep feeder for calves that had been weaned or were in the process of being weaned from their mothers.

"Do you see its plan? The narrow openings in the fence are big enough for the calves to walk through but too small for the cows. Cows like to loaf around where there's shade and water. See the wide eaves that protect the feeder's side troughs and see the doors at either end? They're installed that way so that the person filling the feeder needn't have to go inside. This one will accommodate about thirty calves."

"It's gorgeous!" screamed Buell. "I wish I had one. And some calves. I wish we could have a ranch. I wish I could live here and be a cow hunter." High-fared, adventuring, he said, "Lend me your flashlight a minute, Cam," and went up the fence and over it and ran across the pen to the feeder, pawing the ground, investigating the pen's construction, poking his head into its feed stalls, bawling, pretending to be a hungry calf.

"Oh, for crying in a bucket," said Evelyn and turned her back on the scene. Solemn and old and absolute, the darkening wild met her gaze. Beside her, Camfield set his elbows on the topmost rail of the fence, leaning against it, tilting his head back as if he found in the starred sky some personal fondness.

"Relax," he said. "We've got time to spare. Right about now Lavaliere has just started broiling the Major's supper steaks."

"If I was the one broiling the Major's steaks," said Evelyn, "I'd try calling him too late for his supper and do it often enough so that he'd suffer. I'll bet he doesn't wear half-soled shoes. I'll bet he's got fifty pair and they're all new."

"Did you think to phone Reba to tell her you and Buell were here?" asked Cam.

"Sure," answered Evelyn. "She was waiting on a customer so could only talk a minute though. She sounded like she had a mouthful of gum. Has she taken that up too? I asked her but all she did was laugh. I guess she thinks her being a waitress is funny. I don't."

"Evvie," said Cam, "it isn't written anywhere that the way Reba and I are living now is going to be forever."

"Did I say it was?"

"No, but that's the way you're acting."

"Maybe," said Evelyn, calling forth from a full and disdainful heart a puckish thought, "it's written somewhere that you're going to end up being just like Henry."

Camfield grinned.

"You'd like to be like him?" said Evelyn, angered.

"I didn't say that," said Camfield. And said, "There comes the moon."

"I see it," said Evelyn. Awkward and hopeful and

brilliantly ignorant, she stood apart from the fence, her hands clasped at her back. "Camfield, just before school let out Wilson Padgett got into some new trouble and this time he's been sent away."

"Has he," said Cam, and the wind rising from a fresh place skimmed past the creep feeder, murmuring its dry secrets.

It had to be, Cam's careless indifference to this latest piece of dirt concerning Wilson Padgett, for even in his bad-boy place, even bent now to wills stronger than his own, Wilson was the triumph of his kind and victor over Camfield's.

And it had to be that Evelyn herself soon was to fall victim to the far-reaching resources of the Wilson Padgetts of the world.

Three

GABLED OF ROOF and stately of portal and with the haughty air of old landowner plutocracy, the home of Major Peacock looked as if it had been hauled up out of the ranks of common southern mode by some well-heeled idea. It was spit-and-polish and a foreigner to its surround, this house standing so vain and lighted and classic-white on its extravagant mat of groomed turf. Its flanking gardens looked as if they had been laid out by someone with a mathematical mind, so precise and prim they were. Had a weed ever dared to grow beside their pools and lampposts or beneath their stone benches? Who cared for them? Did the Major's wife give parties in them?

"The Major has a crew of gardeners who come out from Belle Plain regularly," said Cam. "He doesn't have a wife. To my knowledge he never has had. The gardens are one of his whims and so is the use of his front door, so we'll just drive around here to the back and go in through the kitchen. Remember what I told you now. Major Peacock is my employer and you're not to react to how he looks or any of his ways or anything he says with anything but respect. Don't ask him to show you his medals and don't ask him anything personal. He doesn't particularly care for children and only consented to meeting you as a favor to me, so don't talk back to him. If he criticizes Reba or me don't jump in and try to defend us. It'll only be talk. You got all that?"

"We've got it," answered Evelyn. The sight of the Major's house, grander than any she had ever seen, had revived her interest in him. Since hearing Henry's tale her opinion of him was still tilted in his disfavor, but for the moment was of no matter. She wanted a story to take back to Velda Grace Renfroe. Already she had some of it mapped out in her mind: The Major was tall and rangy looking. Like Abraham Lincoln. Sad like him, too, for he had seen thousands of his men die on foreign shores and each of their deaths had been like a knife turned in his heart. The Major never walked in his gardens during the daytime. He only did that when his memories tormented him most. He was a tormented man. Velda Grace would love hearing about that part; she'd slobber over it.

At the Major's back entrance there was a bicycle with an attached metal basket parked up close to the steps, and as Camfield brought the pickup around to a stop he said, "That's Lavaliere's horse." And Buell, ready for the coming greatness, ready to laugh at anything, placed a hand on his belly and shook with silent mirth.

He knew about horses on wheels, marvelous inventions, Buell did. Though he did not own one, Evelyn did and sometimes he was her passenger as she rode through the neighborhood streets, fleeing anywhere, scudding around the sidewalk corners, wheeling through parks and alleyways, pumping, pumping. The thing that would discourage next time hadn't been invented yet. Always after the wild, grim rides, Buell thanked her gravely even as his voice shook and his legs trembled. Little cuckoo.

Buell also knew about kitchens, those plain, glamorous places where the families he knew gathered at suppertime to eat the magic from the stoves and refrigerators and pass the good talk back and forth. But he had never seen a kitchen like that of Major Peacock's and neither had Evelyn. It was as big as the Chestnuts' living and dining rooms combined; its walls were white stone all hung with copper-bottomed cooking utensils; it had a little round table standing off in a corner beneath a window and an immense square one in its middle. Its oven, set as it was, in one of the walls, showed only its glowing glass face. From this Lavaliere was spearing thick, sizzling steaks, plopping them onto a waiting platter. On the big table there stood a great pan of cobbler oozing purple juices.

Lavaliere was in a bad humor. To Evelyn and Buell she said, "Hey, lambs. I see you made it. Impressive, isn't it? Don't it all just give you a pure pity-fit though?"

"Yes," said Evelyn, who had to assume that a pity-fit was one that made you feel sorry for yourself.

"That's the way it affected me when I first came here," said Lavaliere, "but I got over it. You will too if you hang around here long enough, so put your eyes back where they belong, honey." She was arranging the steaks on the platter, spooning their hot liquid fat over the mound of them. To Cam she said, "Nobody knows it yet but I'm going to town with you. I've got the toothache again and this time no aspirin or anything like that is going to do it any good. I've got to go find a dentist, not tomorrow or Monday but tonight. We can stop on the way out and drop Daddy off his supper."

"I hear you," said Cam. He had taken Buell to one of the chairs standing at the little table in the corner and was seating him, trying to soothe his excitement. "We'll go in and see the Major in a minute, but right now let's just sit here quietly."

"Quietly," assented Buell, whispering.

There were three white envelopes on the table and, after glancing them over, Cam lifted one and, without opening it, folded it and tucked it into his shirt pocket. To Evelyn he said, "You might as well come over and join us, old lady."

"I have never had a toothache," said Evelyn, watching Lavaliere scoop cobbler from its pan, plopping a helping of it into a bowl. "But Velda Grace Renfroe, that's a girl I know, had one once. It swelled her whole face up. She eats about two pounds of candy a week. You don't eat candy, do you?"

"I eat what the Major leaves," said Lavaliere, taking up the platter and the bowl. She quit the room and was gone for about five minutes. When she came back through the swinging door she told Cam, "I told him you were here, but wait a little before you go in.

Let him get started. Did you count your pay?"

"No," answered Cam genially, "I didn't. If it's short I'll tell the Major about it later and he'll make it good. Are you going to town with us dressed like that or will we have to wait for you to change when we get to your house?"

"He's cut Daddy's pay," said Lavaliere. "Again. And it's take it or leave it. That's what he said to me, take it or leave it. And do you know what Daddy would say if I didn't hide it from him? If I didn't make up the difference out of my own envelope like I did the last time? He'd say for me to hush my mouth. He'd say the Major and him are friends and ask me where else could we go and be treated so good. My daddy," said Lavaliere, "is a fool and I'm not far behind him. Tim Barnett might have asked me to marry him. I was working on him but now he's gone and that's the Major's fault. Tim was right in his argument. I shouldn't have let him get away. I should have proposed to him. He would have said yes. He'd have taken Daddy and me away from here."

"Tim Barnett," commented Camfield, "is a lot older than you."

"He said he'd write to me," said Lavaliere. "If he does I want you to help me with how I answer back." A spasm of pain went over her face and she slapped a hand to her cheek. "Teeth. You know what the Major told me to do about this one that's killing me? He told me to go out and shoot a squirrel and quick take its liver out and put it in my mouth and hold it there.

He said that's what he used to do when his teeth hurt him."

"Well," said Cam, "how do you know that wouldn't work?" Rising, he motioned to Evelyn and Buell, and the trio went through the swinging door and passed through a small room to a larger one where taxidermied birds with drawn talons, with wild wings stiffly spread, swapped fixed stares from perches and stuffed, antlered heads vied for wall space. Beneath the heads sat Major Peacock taking his supper in the company of two overweight bulldogs, each squatted on the floor, one on either side of the Major's chair. The Major was feeding them, lifting pieces of steak from his plate with his fingers, plopping them into the dogs' wrinkled, waiting mouths. The dogs understood that each was to wait his turn. Only their eyes moved, greedily following each movement of the Major's greasy hand. "Here, Bruno," said the Major. "Here, Junior," and pretended not to notice that he had company until the last piece of meat on his plate was plopped into his own mouth and the dogs lay at his feet in half-stupor, gazing indifferently at the three standing just inside the doorway.

They continued to stand where they were until Major Peacock took up a spoon and drew the bowl of cobbler toward him. With the fourth bite his lips and teeth turned purple and with the fifth one he spoke to Cam. "Hey, Cracker, what you got there?"

"Sir," said Cam, "these are the two children I spoke with you about. This is Evelyn and this is Buell."

53

"Oh, yes," said the Major, again digging into the cobbler. "Your-in-laws." His hair sat on his head like a bushy wheel and was the color of old concrete. None grew over his right ear, which was a hole without the normal trimming, and there was a droop to his right eye. Around and beneath it and the ear hole there ran a wide, pale scar. Ignoring Evelyn and Camfield, talking around the food in his mouth, he leaned forward, eyeing Buell. "Well, young man, you might as well tell me what you're all about."

"I brought you a present!" said Buell in a voice too loud, and bounded forward to sling what was left of his supply of pomander balls onto the Major's table. One of them escaped from the bag and rolled out and dropped to the floor. The dog Bruno jumped, sniffed at the ball and returned to his napping.

Panted Buell, "They're pomander balls. You hang them in your closet and they make your clothes smell good. They don't ever wear out. Camfield taught me how to make them."

"Did he so," parried Major Peacock with dry amusement in his good eye. "Well, I guess that's a good thing as any to be about, pomander balls. They're right pretty and I thank you, though I must say you surprise me, a hefty little fellow like you wasting his time on girl things."

At once Buell's enthusiasm drained. As if the Major had slapped him, he stepped backward until he stood again between Camfield and Evelyn.

Cam's stance was relaxed. On his face there was

54

the expression of one who knew himself to be in a presence more exalted than his own. He was a cow hunter, a keeper of fences and land, come to collect his wages. He was living a life for which he was never intended, but he alone was to blame for this. He stood outside the Major's recognition and his smile was patient and tender, forgiving everyone everywhere everything.

But Buell, not yet ready to be put down entirely, made an announcement. "I am," he declared defensively, "about a lot more than pomander balls. I don't even like them much. They were just a little old something for me to do. I'm not arty. I'm going to be a soldier. There's a man back home who was one and he showed me how to salute. See?" he said and brought his hand up smartly, saluting the Major, thanking him for this brief, disappointing audience.

The Major's return salute was not so snappy. He was finished with Buell and finished with his cobbler and now Evelyn received his attention. He gave it to her but was not really concentrating. "And what about you, sis? Or don't you know yet?"

"I don't know yet," responded Evelyn, giving back to her host only the same surface courtesy being extended to her. She had switched her mind again and decided that she did not, after all, want conversation with the Major, but if forced she would not come off second best as Buell had. "I'm not about anything," she said.

"Is that so," said the Major. "Well, now I'm surprised again. You know what I thought you was going to tell me? That you're a degree person like Cracker there."

"No," said Evelyn. "Right now I'm just living. I'm plain."

"Some of the plainest people I know have got them a college degree or one from a university," said Major Peacock. "I knew a three-star general one time who had two university degrees, but he was so plain that when they took his picture it came out blank."

"I don't like anybody to take my picture," said Evelyn.

"The general didn't either," said the Major, "but they used to sneak up on him and do it anyway."

"If anybody tried to take my picture without me telling him he could I'd clean his plow for him," said Evelyn.

There was a little silence and then Major Peacock said, "How do you like my ranch?"

"It's big," answered Evelyn, unable to think of anything more complimentary.

"Would you like to live on it?"

"No."

"Why not?"

"That's hard to say. All those crawly things out there."

"You afraid of crawly things?"

"No much. They just don't thrill me is all."

"What are you afraid of?"

"Not much."

The Major's face had lighted as if he saw in her something kenful, a flavor that pleased and whetted, a promise. Whimsical and curious, he offered her an experience. "Sis, how would you like to stay here with me and keep me company and let Cracker and the little soldier and Lavaliere go on to town by themselves?"

"I want to see Reba," objected Evelyn. "And I'm hungry."

"You can see Reba later tonight and all day tomorrow," argued Major Peacock. "Cracker will come back for you soon as he gets back from Belle Plain. And there's plenty of groceries here all cooked up nice. You stay here with me and let the others go on to town by themselves. I need somebody like you to talk to." He was Camfield's boss and her patron and, after the others had gone, sat across from her watching her consume a whole steak and part of another. "Them are thoroughbred steaks."

"Good," said Evelyn, licking the bones.

"If you want some cobbler you can go to the kitchen and help yourself. It's kind of gummy."

"I'm full," said Evelyn and sat back wondering what next to expect. She had eaten the way she always ate, fast and with intense concentration, and all the while the Major had played along, making only little offhand comments about nothing, but he was now ready to settle down to business. From the night beyond the windows, from the garden, from the dusk life, there sounded a trailing, migrant note and the Major said, "You like dogs?"

"I do, but my dad won't me have one," said Evelyn. "When Camfield and Reba first got married and lived with us Cam had one. Some boys in his class killed it. That's when he was a teacher."

"You like Cracker, don't you?"

"His name is not Cracker," said Evelyn, counting the stuffed birds. "It's Camfield."

"That don't keep him from being what he is," said Major Peacock, and the left side of his face produced a smile. He said, "You don't favor her much, but in some way you recall to my mind a girl I knew one time when I was soldiering down in the South Pacific. She was one of them wild beggar kids that follow missionaries and soldiers around."

"I never beg anybody for anything and I don't follow anybody around," said Evelyn.

The dog Junior had gone to the French doors overlooking the Major's terrace and was whining to be let out. "He wants to go out," said the Major.

"I think you're right," said Evelyn.

"He can't open the door by himself."

"That must be aggravating. I know how it is to want to do something and can't."

The Major rose, went to the door, opened it and Junior waddled out. Returning to the table and his chair, Major Peacock said, "You hadn't said a thing about how I look. How come?"

"How you look is your business, the same as how I look is mine," said Evelyn.

With a thumb, the Major traced his facial scar.

"A while ago you told me you wasn't about anything. Now, I know that is not hardly the truth. Everybody is about something. You ever thought when you get grown you might join up with the diplomatic corps? Or with one of the military services?"

"No," said Evelyn. "I wouldn't be any good at either one of those things."

"If you was smart you would," said the Major, taking fire from the thought. "If you was smart like I see you are, you could sign on in one of the military services as a recruit and work your way up through the ranks. That's what I did. I didn't go to any college and I didn't go to any university. I was made an officer on the battlefield. Before I was a major I was a lieutenant."

"If I signed on as a recruit they'd have to make me an officer right then and not wait for the battle-field or I wouldn't sign," said Evelyn. "And I'd make them write it down that I wouldn't have to kill any-body either."

"American women don't get sent to battlefields unless they're spies or nurses," said the Major. "That might get changed sometime but right now that's the way it is."

"I wouldn't want to be a nurse," said Evelyn. "Or a spy either. Spying's dangerous. One time I opened a letter that was addressed to my mother. It was from my teacher and afterward I had to go to Grandma Chestnut's every Saturday for three months and do housework. I didn't know how to do it right, so had to do it over about ten times." Remembering and caught up in the honest humiliation of remembering, Evelyn made a ruthless confession. "I still don't know how to do it and I'm not just talking about housework either. It's everything. Everything I do turns out wrong. My mind runs off."

"Runs off where?" asked Major Peacock.

"I don't know where it goes," said Evelyn. "Somewhere. One day I asked somebody why I couldn't do anything right. It was scary."

"Who did you ask?"

"I didn't know who it was. It wasn't anybody I knew."

"When you want answers to private questions like that," advised Major Peacock, "You should go to somebody you know."

"I didn't know I was going to do it," said Evelyn. "It was Theo who caused it. He's not even a year old yet and I know he can't say whole sentences, but one day when I was hauling him over to Grandma Chestnut's in his carriage he raised up and threw his bottle at me and told me I'd better shake out of it."

"Shake out of what?"

"I don't know what he meant. I asked him, but that's all he said. Shake out of it. And he laughed. So when we got to Grandma Chestnut's house she and Grandpa took him across the street to show their neighbors how cute and smart he is, and I went out back of the shed where they keep the wood for their fireplace and got down on my knees and asked somebody why I couldn't ever do anything right."

"And somebody told you?"

"Not right away. I had to wait a minute. But then I heard this voice. It was way off at first. Then it came down to where I was and said, 'You rub me the wrong way.' I waited for it to say some more but it didn't. I don't know who it was."

There was a movement in the Major's thick throat. He leaned forward. "You're a case, aren't you?"

"I guess I am," replied Evelyn.

"The people in Belle Plain say I'm one, but I notice whenever the ladies want somebody special for one of their parties they always invite me. And whenever they get hard up for something quaint to put in their mullet wrapper they send somebody out to snap pictures of my house and cows and take down what I have to say. You ever had your picture in a newspaper?"

"No," said Evelyn. There was no clock in the room and she wondered what time it was and how long it would be before Camfield came back for her.

"Tell me some more about that voice you heard," wheedled Major Peacock.

"There's nothing more to tell," said Evelyn, counting the stuffed birds.

"There was a lad in one of my outfits who heard voices," said Major Peacock. "He was from Montana and could sing in about ten different languages, but if ever he found out the difference between a machine gun and a post-hole digger he kept it to himself. One time those voices of his got to pestering him so bad I had to have him locked up for a few days. After that they quit. When we got through fighting the war and everybody came home, he wrote and asked me for a job and I told him to come on down and I'd put him to work. He knew a little about pasture planning and some of the other stuff that goes with land-use on a ranch, and maybe could have worked himself into a good thing here except he smiled a lot and kept his eyes closed when he talked. So one day I was forced into handing him his walking papers."

"His what kind of papers?" asked Evelyn.

"I fired him," said the Major.

"For smiling? And keeping his eyes closed when he talked? After he'd come all the way from Montana to work for you?" Incredulous, Evelyn set her gaze on the Major's face and then shifted it, counting the stuffed birds again, this time backward. When she got to the one on the end perch she started again but then stopped.

The Major was looking at her with a droll, innocent lift of his brow, and there was no evidence of anything in this, yet comprehension came and she saw how matters with the Major stood. He had pulled Bruno over between his knees and was stroking the animal's ears, and even as Wilson Padgett had talked his way out of wrongdoings, burying them with a schoolboy's sly, fake remorse, said, "Aw, there was more to it than that. Montana didn't fit here. He wasn't like other men, didn't even smell like them. He had too much class. But we don't want to waste our time talking about him. Let's talk about something interesting. You like to fish? How'd you like to go fishing with me come Monday?"

"I might like it," said Evelyn, rising, "but come Monday Buell and I won't be here. We're going home."

"What'd I say?" said the Major. "Did I say something to make you mad? Hey, where are you going?"

"I'm going to borrow Lavaliere's bicycle and I'm going back to Cam's house," answered Evelyn. "If I don't meet him on the way and he comes here first for me you can tell him that's where I am." Made sick by her discovery and afraid that if she stayed longer she would dive into it headfirst, she pulled her lips back from her teeth in imitation of a grin and kept them that way until she was out of the Major's house, until she could no longer see him standing on his terrace waving his puzzled good-bye, until the lights of his garden were behind her and the moon-whitened road was before her.

The prairie night was stealthy, filled with a thousand odors and a thousand shapes, shapes that belonged to this hour. Evelyn looked out at them once but after that stoically kept her eyes fixed on the road and stoically pumped her mechanical steed. The dirt beneath its wheels was hard-packed and she passed the darkened Workmans' cabin without pausing.

Something with goblin wings swooped from a tree and disappeared into the silence. There was dew.

And there, finally, was the ugly little house that was home to Camfield and Reba. Panting, relieved, Evelyn stopped and swung from the bicycle, intending to push it the balance of the way. The wilderness house was unlighted save for a single, bare-bulbed lamp Cam had left burning in its foremost room. There was no activity around the place. The pickup was still gone.

Evelyn started forward but then left the road, pushing the bicycle through sand to a long, irregular stand of fat bushes. When she reached them she went around them and lowered herself and the bicycle to the ground. Knowing that she was completely hidden from view, she laughed. For leaving her with Major Peacock, old jealous phony, old gasbag, Camfield had a scare coming to him. It would scare him silly to go to the Major's house and be told she wasn't there. He'd tear up and down the road looking for her and maybe she'd let him look all night. It would teach him a lesson he wouldn't soon forget.

Savoring this piece of devilment, Evelyn went forward on her knees and after a moment bent to create a little peephole in the thick foliage of the bush nearest her. For her purposes it was perfect and, satisfied, she returned to the ground, but then quickly stood, her attention drawn to a noise coming from the road running past the ranch's perimeter fences. It was a truck, but too quiet to be Cam's and was running without lights. When it reached the gate it turned in and stopped and then its headlights pierced the darkness. A figure on its passenger's side jumped out and in a second was at the gate. It swung open and the truck rolled in, paused long enough to collect the gate opener, and then again it rolled, purring, with no fuss. It was new and big. In the moonlight its body shone. When it passed her hiding place Evelyn saw that a girl was driving it. It traveled a few yards, stopped, moved backward, turned into a field on the opposite side of the road, stopped again. Its lights picked out a huddle of sleeping calves and one by one they started up, sauntering toward the truck. By this time the girl was out of the truck and so was her companion, a man wearing jeans and a Stetson.

In charge, the man said, "See what I told you? There's a right way and a wrong one to do everything. The way I'm showing you is the right one. Once you leave the road, put your lights on and keep them on. If you come up on cattle in the dark they'll run, but if you keep your lights on them they'll come to you."

On her knees at her peephole, Evelyn had both hands over her mouth and was drinking her own breath, aware that she was viewing something plotted and dangerous. Her heart beat a warning.

"T. D. and me was always afraid of the game warden and the state troopers," said the girl.

The man had run around to the back of the truck and lowered its tailgate. He came running back. "If a game warden or a state trooper or somebody like that happens up on you while you're on somebody's property like this you should have a story ready. Say your truck was stolen and you've been out looking for it and you've just now found it. That will explain it being in somebody else's field."

"What if you're asked for some I.D.?" asked the girl.

"When I'm out working like this I never carry any I.D.," answered the man. "The only thing I carry on my person is a little loose money. If we was to be stopped tonight and asked for I.D., I'd say I lost my billfold. It couldn't be proved that I hadn't and it couldn't be proved that I was the one who had put the calves in the truck if I said I found it here all loaded, that somebody stole it from me and I found it here. It would be my word against the lawman's. The most he could get me for would be trespassing. The most important thing in this business to remember is to act like you've got a right to be where you are and doing what you're doing. The important thing is, you've got to work fast and don't let anything slip. Get into the field, get your load and get out. Once you're back on the highway you're pretty safe if you've been careful, if you keep your mind on what you're doing and have your stories ready in case you're questioned and if you don't take any cows with brands. A brand is too easy to spot. Marks are different. When I go into somebody's field for a load the first thing I do is check to make sure I don't pick up anything with a brand on it. If there's a brand, I leave it alone. But if there's only marks to worry about they can be fixed. Did T.D. show you how to do that?"

The girl was standing outside the beam of the pickup's lights but the moon was full on her. She wore a man's loose-tailed shirt. She said, "He tried to one time but botched it."

"T.D. is a loser," said the man, "otherwise he wouldn't be where he is now. An earmark is easy to get rid of but don't tackle it until your calf is tranquilized. Then all you do is cut it out, let the ear bleed a little and then smear it with some cup grease. Give me the gun. Is it loaded?"

"You loaded it yourself," answered the girl.

The calves, all solid red and black except one mottled one, had moved up closer to the truck and the man was walking around them checking their flanks and ears. "Good. Good. No ear tags. No marks. No brands. And none over two-hundred pounds. Everything like Cam promised. He never misses, that boy doesn't. Good." He bent to the mottled calf and gave it a slap. "We don't want you. You might be a favorite of your owner and if we took you he might miss you and start looking for you, and then he might start looking for your buddies here too, so you can go. Go."

Across the road, hidden by her bushes and the lance-tall weeds around them, Evelyn continued to sit and gaze, strangely allured by the scene before her, mercifully made impotent by it. There was a prickle on her scalp and the fine hair on her forearms felt iced.

She saw the man, weapon in hand, move a few feet from the calves. He raised his arm and there was a popping sound and then another and another, six in all, and after several minutes, the calves began to weave and stagger.

When the first of them fell the man was at it immediately, roping its left front leg to its left hind leg. The girl was in the truck, backing it, maneuvering it around to where the drugged animals lay. The tempo of all of this had quickened and now there was no talk.

Supported by both the man and the girl, the calves were dragged over to the truck and then were grasped and lifted and rolled up onto the bed of the truck. The girl was big and backed away from none of it.

When the last of the calves had been loaded, the truck's tailgate was closed, the girl and the man ran around and jumped into its cab, its doors slammed and then again it was in the road. It passed Evelyn and went past the wilderness house and its yellow lights picked out the outline of the gate. And then both its yellow lights and its red ones were absorbed by the night.

The minutes went by and went by and presently Evelyn stood and lifted the bicycle and, pushing it, went across to stand in the place where the rustlers had played their scene. The corrupted grasses had been flattened by hoof and machine and booted feet, but even now they were recovering, slowly straightening, reaching up to drink the falling dew.

Four

How HARD IT WAS then to steal homeward, to sit alone in the dim closes of the ten o'clock kitchen like an old, newly bereaved farm woman. She had to sit for there was no will left in her to do otherwise. She was quiet and did not bend much to the pain in her. There was a longing for Theo and for her parents and for her grandparents Chestnut and Reba. She listened for the sound of Cam's truck and wondered how she would behave when he and the others came.

She had to walk, and went through the little rooms switching on lights, listening and looking for something, for some release, for some random little piece of anything that might help put her back together again.

In one of the rooms, bare of furniture and window dressings, she stood before an unframed canvas propped against the wall. It had been mutilated by some sharp instrument, a knife or scissors, and yet in its glazes, in its unpostured and unlying painted strokes, there was still enough. Its life was still there, lighted like some waiting frontier and the distance of it stretching back, back to the unrevealed. In it there was something too bright to see and what did its destruction mean? Had it been done in a moment of rage or was it a decision?

Curled in her brain, a thought sighed and turned and raised itself and knowingly breathed its truth, and when it had finished speaking she was sure. The destruction of the painting had been a decision. Everything now pointed to that. And it had been made by Cam, helped along by all those others who either couldn't or wouldn't understand. The fact was, they had never seen a pink bird or a blue prince much less ever tried to paint one. The fact was, they had never stopped long enough to look at any bird or listen to one, never made a dream, only wanted everything solved without fuss or harm or attention themselves. Anything that got in the way of their methods, so safe and planned, had to disappear because their brains could do no better for them. And because they couldn't, they would never change.

But not Camfield. Camfield was away out front. Changeable. Too much over everybody else's head. And only because he was so, only because he had struck out too much, had said too much, expected too much, had he been forced out.

Defending these thoughts and then, as she sometimes closed a book on a chapter that was harsh and said too much, asked too much, she closed her mind to all of them and all related to them and returned to the kitchen where she sat waiting and listening for the return of the others.

Night of deceit, reckless and wonderful, with

everybody crowded around the table eating Evelyn's cake, the laughter sometimes ringing to the ceiling and the hungry, eager talk tumbling so fast that some of the words were lost.

Said Cam to Evelyn, "But why didn't you wait for us at the Major's house? We took the other way in, thinking that's where you'd be."

"What other way in?" asked Evelyn.

"The Major has his own private entrance road," explained Reba. "It's off limits to his hired hands but tonight we used it."

"The dentist stuck Lavaliere with a horse needle," chattered Buell. "It was a foot long and he fixed her tooth, but when we got back to the Major's house Reba and Cam and me had to clean up his kitchen because Lavaliere felt bad and then we took her to her house. That's what took us so long. Mr. Jim can speak Greek."

Reba had exchanged her long, smooth hairstyle for one that was short and spiral-curled and her lips were no longer pink and sweet but painted a dark, flaunting red. "Tell me about home," she said.

"Well," said Evelyn, "it's still there and everybody wants to know when you and Camfield are coming back. When are you? Ever? Never?"

"Oh," said Cam, "we'll be back one of these days. As soon as we get enough money saved so that when we get there we'll be able to afford a real house and a few acres. Maybe I'll turn farmer." He was watching Reba, who had finished her cake and was emptying the pockets of her orange waitress uniform, placing the green bills and stacking the coins on the bare table with all the seriousness of a fussy child, for Reba was the kind that had to know the exact. How many miles from here to there, how many more ounces in the larger jar than in the smaller one, how many nails in a pound, what hour, what place, what size. "Reba thinks she'd like being a farmer's wife," said Cam.

"Grandpa still has his pecan trees and his chickens," said Buell. "But when he wants a chicken to eat he goes to the store and buys it. He won't let anybody kill any of his. He's got a new rooster named Ernest and takes it for walks. On a leash."

"We still have to go to Grandma's every Sunday for dinner," said Evelyn. "And Dad still has to churn the ice cream on the back porch. Grandma won't let anybody else. She says if anybody else does it, it comes out sloppy."

"She let me do it once," said Reba. "I thought my arm was going to drop off before I finished. What color is Grandma's hair now?"

"Yellow," said Buell. "Except sometimes she makes it black."

"Grandma and her hair," said Reba. "I remember the time she was going to teach me to curl it with a curling iron. She wouldn't let me give her a permanent. She wanted me to use her curling iron so we got it out and heated it and I tried it."

"On me!" cried Evelyn. "You tried it out on me

first and let the iron get so hot the first curl came off with it. It was fat and when you looked at it you turned so white Grandma shoved a chair under you. It was funny."

In purest delight Buell watched his sisters, and the talk and the fun and the remembering of things that had been when the family was all together went on and on.

During a lull in the conversation Camfield said to Evelyn, "You never did tell us why you didn't wait for us at the Major's house."

"I got tired," explained Evelyn, "so I borrowed Lavaliere's bicycle and came on back here. Had a good ride. Saw a bat. He almost ran into me. Didn't see any cows though. Will you take Lavaliere's bike back to her in your truck or are you going to make me do it? She'll need it if she goes to the Major's house tomorrow morning to cook his breakfast."

"I'll get it back to her tonight or early tomorrow morning," said Cam. "Don't worry about it."

Far into the night he and Reba talked behind their closed door, their voices rising and falling. From time to time there was hushed laughter. Buell slept and beside him Evelyn lay upon her back gazing at the square of moonlighted window. Reality returned, the memory of the rustling she had witnessed of which Cam was a part, and she rose once and looked out but there was nothing of import to note.

The wild of the prairie stretched away and away and on it nothing moved. In her ordinary experience she was not an expert on clouds, yet knew enough about them to know that the long delicate trails riding eastward meant good weather for the approaching day.

It came without a murmur, hot again and still. In the Sunday dawn she woke with a start. She was alone in the bed and beyond the frame of the uncurtained windows the great horizontal daylight scenery greeted her startled eyes. Startled they were because she had managed several hours of sleep. There was a tussle with her clothes, the same ones she had worn the day before. She hurried past the bathroom without a pause.

In the kitchen Buell sat placidly forking scrambled eggs into his mouth. He was freshly bathed and freshly dressed and was full of wise truths. "You smell. How come you don't wash when you get up like I do?"

"Because," said Evelyn, "I don't want to look like an old truck by the time I'm fifteen. Too much washing takes all of the natural oils out of skin. Where is everybody?"

"Cam's gone to take Lavaliere's bicycle to her," reported Buell. "He has to work till noon and Reba's not going to get up till she feels like it. Cam put your eggs and toast in the oven. Probably they're cold by now."

"Food is food," said Evelyn, peppering the cold eggs on the cold plate.

Bright and stainless in his past and present, Buell watched her eat. "A man phoned."

Evelyn swallowed a bite of toast. "What did he say?"

"I couldn't hear what he said. Cam talked to him."

"Well, what did Cam say?"

"He told whoever he was talking to that everything was fine. Then he hung up and told me a joke. Want me to tell it to you?"

"No. Buell, I want to tell you something and I don't want you to scream."

"Tell me what?" said Buell, instantly suspicious.

"Tomorrow," said Evelyn, "I think we'd better go on back home."

"Home!" screamed Buell. "But we just got here yesterday."

"Hush. I told you not to scream. Listen. Because of the way things are, Reba and Camfield don't have much time to spend together now and we're in their way, so tomorrow we'd better go back home. We can stay with Grandpa and Grandma till Mama and Dad get back from St. Louis."

"You can go home if you want to," said Buell, "but I'm going to stay here."

"We're in the way, Buell."

"How?"

"You little yahoo. Can't you see how? Should I draw you a picture?"

"Of what?"

"Of how we're in the way."

"We aren't in the way. Reba and Camfield both love us and we love them."

"Don't give me a bad time, Buell. I'm your boss now and I say tomorrow we should go home."

The nature of Buell, sturdy and tender and visionary, proclaimed itself. "All right. We'll go. But when we get there Grandpa and Grandma will want to know why we came back so quick and we'll have to say because Reba and Cam don't have much time together now, and they'll want to know why and then we'll have to tell them about Reba working for Mr. Jim at The Orange Blossom Cafe and how she only comes home on Saturday nights—and they'll think that's not right and then they'll worry. Everybody will worry. Can I have some coffee?"

"No," answered Evelyn, pushing the word from her mouth with her tongue.

"We going home tomorrow?"

"No."

"You switched your mind?"

"Yes."

Generous in his victory and serene again, Buell said, "I just love Camfield, don't you, Evvie?"

"Yes," replied Evelyn, feeling five years old again. And dealing in something beyond her history, something for which she knew no terms, said, "But listen, Buell. Listen to me. Not either of us should love him too much."

Buell licked a little ooze of butter from his knife.

"He'll be back a little after noon. What should we do till then?"

"I don't know," said Evelyn. "Sit here and stare at each other until one of us goes blind, I guess."

"I'll tell you the joke now," offered Buell.

"Tell it, tell it," groaned Evelyn.

"It's about farmer number one and farmer number two," said Buell. "Number one went to town with twelve ducks. He was going to take them to the zoo. But his truck broke down. So when he saw farmer number two he said, 'Hey, my truck's broke down and my ducks want to go to the zoo. Will you take them for me?' "

"Where was this?"

"Where? I don't know. Somewhere."

"They don't have ducks in zoos. They're too common."

"Evvie, the ducks wanted to go there."

"All right. Maybe it was a different kind of zoo. Did farmer number two take them to it?"

"Yes."

"And that's the joke?"

"No."

"You said you were going to tell me a joke."

"I am if you'll let me."

"Tell it, tell it."

"It's about farmer number one and farmer number two," said Buell. "Number one went to town one day with twelve ducks. He was going to take them to the zoo. But his truck broke down. So when he saw farmer number two he said, 'Hey, my truck's broke down and my ducks want to go to the zoo. Will you take them for me?' So farmer number two put the ducks in his truck and went off to the zoo. About an hour later farmer number one was coming out of the garage where he had got his truck fixed and he saw farmer number two again. Him and all the twelve ducks were walking down the street looking in the windows. So farmer number one ran across to where farmer number two and all the ducks were and said, 'Hey, I thought you said you'd take those ducks to the zoo for me.' Farmer number two had him a big juicy hamburger and he was eating it and he said, 'I took your ducks to the zoo just like I promised you I would and we had some money left over, so now we're going to go to the movies.' "

"I don't think they'd let twelve ducks into a theater," said Evelyn after a moment. "I don't think they'd even let one in. You know how much they charge for movies? You know how much one costs?"

"A hundred dollars," gasped Buell, overcome. He was on the floor with one hand pressed to his abdomen and the other covering his mouth and was rolling and heaving.

"Quit," said Evelyn. "Nothing's that funny. Quit, I said. Somebody's coming." To reach the door she had to step over Buell. She pushed the screened door open and went out onto the porch.

Traveling fast, a closed, late model Jeep occupied the road leading out of the woods and palm hammocks. When it reached a point parallel to the house it slammed to a stop and Major Peacock stepped from it. Gleaming authority and energy, he said, "Howdy, kid."

"Howdy, yourself," said Evelyn. She advanced to the edge of the stoop, sat down on its top step and waited for the Major to tell her that a state trooper had caught the rustlers with their load of stolen calves and that another trooper was on his way out from town to get Camfield. Her heart felt as if someone might have tied a rag around it, fashioning a slowly tightening noose.

Still in the road, the Major leaned against his Jeep. "Where's Cracker?"

"If you mean Camfield," growled Evelyn, "he's out seeing about your fences and your cows. There's nobody here but Buell and Reba and me and Reba's asleep. Was there something special you wanted?"

"No," said the Major. "Nothing special. I always take me a little ride around the place on Sundays checking up on things while they're kind of quiet. Weekdays there's too much going on, and if there's anything wrong the men hide it from me. You and the little soldier still got your minds set on going home?"

"We've been talking about it," said Evelyn, enduring the Major's interested examination. He was regarding her as if he might see in her some kind of strange wealth. Embarrassed and unable to think of anything more productive, she said, "I've got a girl friend back home and I miss her. We're very close."

The Major squatted beside the Jeep and with a forefinger drew a figure eight in the dirt. "If you could give it a few more days maybe you'd find a friend here."

"Friends aren't so easy to make," said Evelyn. "They take a long time."

"Naw they don't," said Major Peacock. "Sometimes it don't take but an hour or so. Why, just look at you and me. Already we're friends and we was only introduced last night. How come you don't like it here?"

Evelyn put her head back and stared at the sky. Its early day colors had melted and now it was baby blue, a clear-eyed reality. "I don't know," she said. "I think the trouble might be Camfield."

"What about him?" said the Major, instantly and defensively alert.

Evelyn brought her head back to its natural position. A young seed was sprouting in her brain, sending out little fruitful tendrils. Loathing the Major's scarred face, loathing more his invisible scars, his bloated vanity and touchiness, his way of knocking others down to make himself look bigger, she produced an accurate frown and, following a roundabout wile, lying again, said, "He's so different than what he used to be. So grouchy and gripey now. Everything gets on his nerves. He didn't say so but I don't think he likes cows and I don't think they like him."

"Well," said Major Peacock, "the job don't call for either side to get chummy with one another."

"He's not a cow man," insisted Evelyn.

"He's a good employee," said the Major.

"He doesn't belong here," said Evelyn. And in a quick, faraway voice said, "If I owned this place and he worked for me I'd give him his walking papers."

"I think you must have got up on the wrong side of the bed this morning like I do sometimes," said the Major tolerantly. "What say you and I take a little ride? It'll take the sting out of whatever it is you're mad about and help you too. I got a show calf I'm fitting out to be a winner and I'd like to get your opinion of him."

"And another reason I don't like it here," said Evelyn, "is it's too dark at night. At home we live on a dark road but all up and down it in front of our house we've got those bluish green lights that come on as soon as it gets dark. They shut off when it gets morning. The electric company put them in. They keep burglars away. Burglars don't like lights. They like it where it's dark." Returning the Major's steady look, Evelyn sucked her lower lip. The world was so wide and demanded so much.

Major Peacock had risen and was studying the road. "Before Cracker and Reba hired on with me I thought about putting in some lights out here. The week before they came, some highbinders slipped in here one Saturday night and relieved me of some saddles and a couple of horses and I reckon about eight beeves. They had to go inside one of the barns after the saddles and horses. At that time we wasn't locking the barns. Cracker noticed it and told me about it, so now we lock all barns come evening. See what I mean about him being a good employee?"

Clumsily and faintly Evelyn asked, "What happened to the highbinders?"

"All but one of them got away clean," answered the Major. "The one that didn't wasn't experienced enough. He's in the jug now. I put him there."

"You put a whole man in a jug?" said Evelyn. "How?"

"Jug is another word for prison," said the Major. "I forgot I was speaking to a lady or I wouldn't have used it. What about that little ride now? I want to show you my prize bull and then I thought we'd jaunt on into town and see about a few things. Where's the little soldier?"

"He's inside," responded Evelyn. And said, "It's too dark out here at night. At home I always take a little walk after supper, but here I can't because there aren't any lights. It looks to me like you'd want this place lighted. If it was, the cow stealers or whatever you call them would be afraid to come."

"They're afraid to come now," returned Major Peacock. "Since Cracker came I haven't been victimized once. He don't lay down on the job like the last one I had living in this house. When he hears a noise he gets up and goes outside and investigates. Holler and tell the little soldier you're going to take a little ride with me. We'll bring him back a little present from town."

"He doesn't want anything from town," said Evelyn, "and if we're going home tomorrow I don't have time to take a ride with you. I have to pack up all our stuff and I guess I should take a bath."

Showing a touch of irritation, the Major put his hands behind his back. "I didn't say I wouldn't put lights in out here. Did you hear me say I wouldn't?"

"I didn't hear you say one way or another," said Evelyn. "And I don't care one way or another. I only mentioned the lights because you asked me how come I didn't like it here."

"You drive a strong bargain, don't you?"

"I don't know what you mean. Not any of this place is a bargain."

"Would it look better to you if I was to arrange with the power company to come out here and put some lights up and down this road?"

"I wouldn't want anybody to think it was my idea," said Evelyn, hoping for a cloudburst or for one of the Jeep's tires to go flat. "Because that wouldn't be the truth, would it?"

"No," said the Major with a sly old eye.

"It was your idea, wasn't it?"

"It sure was."

"So you wouldn't have to explain it to anybody, would you?"

"I sure wouldn't," said the Major. His color was high and his natural eye sparkled.

"When would you have it done? Tomorrow?"

"I'll see about it tomorrow," agreed Major Peacock at once. "I can't guarantee I can get it done to-morrow, but I'll call up and see about it." All eagerness now, he went around the Jeep and climbed in it, fitting himself under the driver's wheel. He leaned and beckoned. "Well, you coming? Come on, we've got things to do."

The noose around her heart had fallen away and yet, curiously, it still felt trapped. And scarred, as if some injury had been done to it. With effort she said, "I'm coming, but you've got to give me a minute." And with effort she rose and went back into the house.

Buell had pulled a step stool over to the kitchen sink and was standing on it washing the breakfast dishes. Without a glance in her direction he said, "Good-bye. I hope you have a good time. I'm glad I wasn't invited. I wouldn't have gone anyway. I don't like him. I thought you didn't."

"You don't know how to think," flared Evelyn. "But I do and so I have to go with Major Peacock." Never had she loved Buell so much and never had she been so envious of him. His little world was so beautiful, so pure and calm, so innocent. Her anger faded and she said, "I have to."

"Yuh," said Buell. "Yuh. Yuh."

Five

THE MAJOR LET IT be known to Evelyn that he had conquered the art of Jeep handling. He drove fast and with skill, cutting away from the road after a mile or so to run up onto an elevation dotted with oak hammocks.

The Jeep was new and air-conditioned and, like a happy, overgrown hound yapping for favor, the Major wasted not a moment on silence. "The June rains haven't started yet. They're late this year. But you just wait till they get here. Then you'll see big, black, mean mosquitoes out here. The first time one gets his tweezers into you you'll think you've been shot."

"Mosquitoes don't mess around with me," said Evelyn. "My grandfather says I'm not natural."

The Major cast a delighted, sidelong look. "Does he think you're unnatural?"

"He didn't say and I didn't ask."

"Weren't you curious?"

"About what?"

"About you being unnatural."

"No. I don't think about what I am. I just live."

"After we have a look at my bull we're going to speed on into town," said the Major. "I got a new name picked out for you and you need some puncher boots and a puncher hat to go with it."

"What new name?" asked Evelyn.

"Aw now," said the Major. "Don't go getting your back up. It's just a little fun thing I dreamed up this morning while I was shaving. It fits you, but if you don't like it we can always change it to something else."

"Tell me what it is," said Evelyn. "As long as it isn't Princess or Sweet Thing or any name like that, I'll like it." Braced for anything because across the Major's face there had come a romantic, starry look, she clung to the armrest on her side of the Jeep's passenger seat.

"It's The Kissimmee Kid," answered Major Peacock and turned his head to show her his harmless and comical smile.

Relief pumped through her. She released her hold on the armrest and settled back. "I don't need a puncher hat or anything else puncher to go with that name. It's enough all by itself. Besides it's Sunday. The stores will all be closed."

"The one we're going to won't be," said the Major. "I own it and the man who runs it for me always does his janitor work on Sundays."

"Where's the dairy part to this joint?" asked Evelyn, peering.

"I don't keep a dairy herd," answered Major Peacock. "And my beef cows only produce enough milk to feed their calves. What size shoe do you wear?"

"Eight," said Evelyn, resigned. "Ten. Twelve. I don't know. When I need new ones I just tell the man to fit me with a pair that won't cripple me for life and he does. He says I've got a good understanding."

"A good understanding," chortled the Major and slapped his knee. "Haw, that's a good one." The oaks were behind them now and they were descending to be met again by flat, grassland province. There were sand sloughs and sand ponds, a slow, wet creek, water tanks and water holes, silos and wandering cattle. They passed a roofed, open-air building with a long squeeze chute and pens jutting from its body, and the Major, taking a stab at explaining this structure, said, "It's a corral. Cattle have to be branded and marked and vaccinated and have to have their blood tested for Bang's disease and tuberculosis, and they've got to be dipped and sprayed for ticks. So when it's time to do these jobs the men round up the beeves and send them through the corrals. You didn't know that, did you?"

"I didn't know any of it," said Evelyn, wanting out of the Jeep, wanting to be rid of the Major, wanting yesterday and today and tomorrow to be wiped out. She wondered what the Major would do if she jumped into his lap and bit the end of his nose off. Would he then, Oh please God, order Camfield to take himself and all of his relatives and go?

She remained calm and stern and the Major continued to drive and talk. They reached a penned, isolated pasture containing a shelter and the promised bull. He was black and appeared restless and impudent and, standing outside the pen beside her, Major Peacock said, "We won't go in because he don't know me yet. I only got him a few days ago and Henry Workman is training him. Henry's already got him halter broke. Isn't he a beauty though?"

"If you like bulls I guess he is," said Evelyn. "I don't know anything about them. I don't know anything about ranches."

Into the Major's face there came a rambling look, the same kind that Buell wore when driven by one of his little yearnings to confess a hidden trouble or some shortcoming. Said the Major, "Well, that's no sin. The business of ranching can't be learned in one day or even one year. I found that out. I wasn't born into the cattle business like most of the other ranchers around here. It was wished off onto me." The roving in his face halted. "Kid, how far you reckon we've come this morning?"

"From Camfield's house to here?" said Evelyn. "I don't know. Is your bull there like a dog? Can you pet him?"

"Never make a pet out of a show calf," said the Major. "That spoils him and gives him bad habits. I wasn't talking how far we came in miles. I was referring to our friendship."

"Our friendship," said Evelyn. "Well, I think we've come a long way in that. Far enough, anyway."

"There's a lot of years between our ages," commented Major Peacock, watching the bull.

"They don't make any difference," babbled Evelyn. "Except you might die before I do, but maybe they'll find a cure for that pretty soon. Do you take vitamins? You ought to. They'd help to keep you healthy and young. My mother gives Buell and Theo and me vitamins every day. Where's your mother? She ought to be here taking care of you." Certain that the Major was about to propose some kind of awful, permanent relationship, she took a step backward. There was a sound as of the dragging of chains in her ears.

The Major had left off observing the bull, who was ambling back to his shelter, and had turned his head, looking at her as if she might have turned into a big, friendly rabbit, all ears. Confidingly he said, "My mother. I want to tell you about her. Her name was Johnny Mae Peacock."

"Was?"

"Was. She died while I was off down in the South Pacific helping to win World War Two. She didn't have any training in it but was good at nursing, and she married Emmett Slaughter a year before he cashed in. He was sick when she married him and they had a deal and he kept his end of it and that's how come I'm a cattle rancher now. I never met Emmett, but the way people tell it he had plenty of class to go along with his plenty of money. They don't say Johnny Mae was class, but she was. She didn't go further than the seventh grade in school, but she had class. It was only her name that didn't fit. Her name didn't fit her."

"Mothers and fathers ought to be more careful

about the names they hang on their children," said Evelyn.

The Major said that he agreed with her and at Peacock's Western Clothing Store in town introduced her to the peevish, fidgety clerk as The Kissimmee Kid.

"Is that so," said the clerk without a flicker of interest and went back to his sweeping and straightening and dusting.

"Don't mind him," said the Major. "He was born mad at the world and never recuperated."

The store was overcrowded with racks hung with clothing and tables stacked with clothing and shelves choked with boxes and showcases displaying leather items.

"Half of the battle of cattle ranching is looking the part," joked the Major, pawing, discarding, selecting. And presently Evelyn stood outfitted to his satisfaction. Inside the boots her feet were surprisingly comfortable, though they kept slipping backward toward the boots' heels. Her cowgirl hat was tall and soft and doe-colored with a black suede band and a curled brim. "You need you a cowgirl shirt and a cowgirl skirt too," said Major Peacock, "but there's nothing here in your size. Oh well, we got what we came for and there'll be another day. You hungry? I got a couple of dollars that says let's you and me go find some chicken and dumplings."

"No," wheezed Evelyn, "I've got to go home now. I promised Buell I'd be back by noon. Sometimes he plays with matches when he gets bored and I wouldn't want him to burn the house down." There was not a syllable of truth in this. Buell never played with matches. "Uh," said Evelyn. "Uh." And, carrying her old shoes, moved to the front of the store.

On his way to the back of the store to empty a wastebasket the clerk met her and paused long enough to offer several comments. "You should have made him buy you a cap. Caps stay on better than hats when you're busting a bronc or when there's a wind. Hats like wind."

"If there's one thing I'm not going to do it's bust a bronc," said Evelyn, blankly gazing at the clerk. She thought that busting a bronc might be something like busting a coconut, but couldn't imagine what wind and hats and caps might have to do with that.

"A bronc is a horse that hasn't been tamed yet," said the clerk.

Evelyn leaned against a counter and watched Major Peacock, who had decided to treat himself to a new hat. He was on a ladder searching an upper shelf for the right color and size. "Lester, hadn't you got anything but black in my size? I want one the same color as The Kid's."

"Want is his middle name," said the clerk. He set the wastebasket down and knelt before Evelyn, squeezing the toes of her boots with a thumb and forefinger. "By the time you get home you'll be used to them," he said, "and won't feel like you're going to fall backward with every step you take."

On the return trip to the ranch Evelyn put her feet flat on the Jeep's floorboard. The boots were leather lined and inside them her feet had begun to feel fevered. She decided that eventually the boots would be a gift to Velda Grace Renfroe. The thought of Velda Grace, so meek and always so willing, brought an ache.

The Major seemed not to notice her discomfort. He said that he felt good, that it made him feel young to be out with a friend on a Sunday morning, everything so peaceful, no trouble anywhere, just the big land and the people on it, tending to their own business. He said that one time some of the people living on the Kissimmee Prairie had called themselves "the pancake people." They were the ones, he said, who had come from places where there were hills and mountains and to them the prairie had looked like a pancake.

"I make good pancakes," said Evelyn. "If I come to visit you again next Saturday night when Camfield and Buell go after Reba I'll make you some for your dessert if you want me to. Back home on Saturday nights we always have pancakes. It's my favorite night of the whole week. At home on Saturday nights I always take a long walk by myself after supper. That's when I get rid of everything that bothers me. I never let anybody go with me. I just walk and think. You'll have those road lights in by next Saturday night, won't you?"

"I will if I can get whoever's in charge of road

93

lights at the electric company to listen to me," answered the Major. "But you mean to tell me I got to wait till next Saturday night before our next date? I thought tomorrow you'd ride around with me and help me boss all the doings. The men will be coralling some of the herds and doing some planting. It's better than going to a picture show. You wouldn't like that?"

"I'd like it," gabbled Evelyn, reeling off her excuses. "But when Buell rides in a car he gets sick and throws up. And I can't leave him home by himself because besides liking to play with matches he likes screwdrivers. He likes to take things apart and then can't get them back together again. Neither can anybody else."

The Major had an immediate and selfishly eager solution. "The little soldier can stay with Lavaliere tomorrow. I'll tell her."

"My dad would make sausage meat out of me if I left Buell with a stranger while I went off to have a good time myself," said Evelyn, and was pleased to see the Major's silly disappointment. When he pulled the Jeep up to Camfield's back steps and stopped, she grabbed her old shoes and jumped from the vehicle with only a cried, "Thanks for everything." Only when she reached the safety of Camfield's kitchen did she remember her burning feet.

Secure, resourceful and contented in his unthreatened world, Buell was seated at the table. Spread before him was an array of artist's supplies, and on a small white canvas he had painted what might have passed for a goat except that the humor that should have been in the animal's face was missing and it had giraffe legs.

Evelyn thudded to the nearest chair and lowered herself into it. The room had sun in it, the clock on the shelf above the sink ticked, the windows were open, the thrum of insects reached her ears. It was all so common and yet she had the feeling that none of it was, that she was being shown something. She removed the new hat and hung it on the post of her chair. The boots required some tugging to get them off.

"I wanted to paint some pink birds but there isn't any pink paint, so I painted this dog," remarked Buell. "What kind do you think he is?"

"That's a dog?" said Evelyn. "I thought it was a goat or a giraffe. You don't know how to paint. Where's Reba?"

"Gone."

"Gone where?"

"Back to town."

"But she wasn't supposed to have gone back until tonight."

"I know it, but Mr. Jim phoned and said he needed her to do some special things for him so when Camfield got home he took her. He's going to bring back some fried chicken and potato salad so we can go to the woods and have a picnic. He let me help him feed and water Spirit. His breath doesn't smell good but he's a nice horse." Dreaming, cuddling his smile, Buell dipped his ungifted brush and added a

95

wanderweed to his square of canvas. "There. Now the goat or the giraffe will have something to eat. It's a dog though. Camfield thinks it is."

"He told you that?"

"Yes."

"He was telling you that to make you feel good," said Evelyn, cold in sudden hostility.

"No," said Buell.

"Buell, he was! Anybody can see that's not a dog. It's a giraffe or a goat. Cam is an artist and he knows the difference."

Buell ducked his chin and showed her a piece of the stuff of which life is made, how its paths are formed, how his own were now being touched and turned, swaying toward another, more attractive and dangerous ground. Adoring, worshipful, his own creature for now, he said, "Camfield never tells anybody anything just to make them feel good. He never lies. He never does anything bad. When he starts up his farm I'm going to live with him every summer and I'm going to watch everything he does so I can be like him."

"You little cuckoo," said Evelyn after a moment. "You dumb little cuckoo."

Standing under the shower in the bathroom, she soaped her hair and body twice while wrestling with thoughts and passions, so many and so mixed that she could not sort through to a clear ending to any of them. In a fury of frustration she moaned once.

She thought of the bird who had sung to her the day before, and when Camfield returned from town with the boxed picnic lunch she was ready. The day had passed its zenith; the sun was now in its westering curve yet still its blaze remained strong and hot and the prairie, sighing and simmering, breathed it.

In a frenzy to get to the woods where her little feathered caroler lived, Evelyn loped ahead of Buell and Camfield. It had been her decision to carry the thermos jug filled with iced tea, and though it was heavy she did not feel its weight. Its wooden handle was a little broken and cut into her hand, but she did not feel the slight hurt of this. The bird would be where he had been the day before. Or he would come. And he would sing again but this time not only for her. This time Camfield would hear its song and then he would know what the bird knew and he would laugh in the old, good way. Or maybe he'd cry. If he cried she would pretend not to see. Neither would she let Buell see.

On reaching the wood she spotted the right tree and sat under it, but did not immediately look for the bird because this was something that should not be hurried. It was too valuable for hurry, too pure. So wait. Be quiet. *Shhhh*.

Under her tree Evelyn crouched and hugged herself and smelled the delicious smell of old roots and old dirt. She stood and watched Camfield and Buell come toward her, and when they were within eye-to-

97

eye distance she made a silencing sign. They came up to her and she leaned forward, whispering, "*Shhhhhh.* Don't talk. I want you to see my bird and if we talk he'll fly away."

"What bird?" said Buell, forming his question only with his mouth, without sound.

"Be quiet. Don't talk. Don't move. Just listen. He'll be here in a minute and you'll hear him. I saw him yesterday. Look up there. That's where he was yesterday and that's where he'll be again today, I just know it. Watch. Listen."

So they stood, watching and listening. And eerily the bird came and, with his bright, liquid eyes unblinking, looked down from his bough and again sang his knowledge, his prayer, his hope. And again, as before, when he had finished he flashed upward and was gone.

"There," said Evelyn. She whirled and with her hands took hold of Camfield's shirtfront with such force that he was pulled toward her. "There. You saw him and you heard him, so what do you think now?"

"He was pretty," offered Buell.

"I think all birds are pretty," said Camfield, pulling his shirt from Evelyn's grasp.

"You think what?" shrieked Evelyn. "What did you say?"

"I said I think all birds are pretty. There are lots of them out here."

"I didn't ask you about all birds! I asked you about that one. I asked you what you thought now!"

Said Camfield, "I think we ought to have our picnic now."

"Our picnic? That's what you think? But didn't you see what I saw? Didn't you see what I saw? The bird? Didn't you hear what he said?"

"Evvie, I saw him. I heard him. I liked him. I like all birds. They're all pretty and they all sing."

"Listen!" cried Evelyn. "Listen. You didn't hear him, what he said." Wild-eyed, beside herself, she put her fingers in her hair and yanked a handful of it backward. "Listen. What he said could make every-thing different for you and Reba. Better and differ-ent!"

"Evvie," said Camfield, "you mustn't worry for a minute about Reba and me. We're doing fine and we're going to do better just as soon as I can get all my plans put together. Let's have our picnic now. Where are the napkins? Did we forget to bring salt? Boy, look at these green onions."

There were the onions and the chicken, the po-tato salad and small, fried apple pies and the iced tea, sweet with sugar and sour with lemon. Camfield said that during one of his years at college he had shared a room with a Japanese student who had regarded the southern American way of preparing tea as uncivilized.

"I don't see anything uncivilized about iced tea," said Evelyn.

"It's good," said Buell.

"Why did your Japanese friend think it was un-civilized?" asked Evelyn.

"We boil it to make a hot," said Camfield. "And put ice in it to make it cold. We put sugar in it to make it sweet and lemon in it to make it sour." He bent and touched her cheek with a finger. "You have eyes like Reba's and they're wonderful, do you know that?"

Evelyn produced a thorny smile. "I guess they're all right. The main thing is, I can see out of them. This morning Major Peacock told me he was going to put lights on that road that runs past your house. The vapor kind. He's going to have it done this week."

"Well," said Camfield, "that sounds like a winner except that if he actually goes ahead with it this time I'll have to buy dark shades for our windows, otherwise there'll be no sleep for any of us. I can't sleep with light streaming in my windows, can you?"

"Lights don't bother Buell and me when we go to bed," said Evelyn. "If they bother you, you could paste some paper on your windows or tack some cardboard over them." She chewed onion, and the sense of problem, of crowding, the anxiety and fear and confusion fell away. Seized by a stronger current, she looked out across the prairie to the road, the one used by the Saturday-night cow stealers. Now it would be closed to them. They wouldn't dare to come in on the lighted road. And no matter for now that Camfield had closed his eyes and his ears to her bird. There would come another, better hour when he would see it and hear it and then those things that had changed him would go away and he would come back and be himself again, be himself again.

Infected with hope and intoxicated with a slow, swelling belief, Evelyn shared her grin with Camfield and helped herself to another onion.

Six

Luxuriously the hope and belief lasted throughout the balance of the day and evening, and then it was night and time again for bed and sleep.

On her back in the double bed in the warm, stuffy room Evelyn drifted in and out of sleep. Curled on the far side of the bed, Buell held queer, garbled bits of conversation with his dream companions—Theo, Grandpa Chestnut and somebody or something named Tooter.

There was palest light at the windows and on the roof a scratching sound as of a small animal. And in the deepest hour of the night there was Camfield's voice on the other side of the closed door, a cautious whisper, asking, "Are you all right in there? Are you asleep?"

The questions, so cherishing, so protective, so big-brotherly, roused Evelyn. She opened her eyes but did not move or speak. She wanted to hear the questions again and in an ecstasy of waiting held her breath.

The questions did not come again. The little animal on the roof was gone and there were Cam's footsteps, furtive, retreating.

Evelyn sat up and, after straightening her pajamas, padded to the door and opened it. Save at its far end where it angled to meet the kitchen, the hallway was black. The door to the bathroom was ajar; she could make out its white fixtures. She went past it and stopped, listening.

Camfield was in the kitchen using the telephone, having a conversation with someone named Quinby, talking fast, saying, "Quinby? Listen, Quin. You won't be able to use the road in front of my place anymore. He's going to install lights this week. Well, my information is secondhand, but I assume he'll light the gate too. He's had this idea before and I suppose he just decided to do it. No, no. Everything's normal. Everything's fine. I just thought you should come prepared for the lights. Well look, Quin, come in above my place. You don't need a gate. You know how to get a fence down and back up in a hurry."

Evelyn waited to hear no more. Afraid that the snarls and wails gathering inside her would escape and burst from her mouth, fantastically afraid that she might faint or fall over dead before she could get back to her room, she made her tiptoe way back to it and again lay beside Buell. She was bitterly lonely and ashamed and disgraced and defeated. All ahead promised nothing. Camfield was lost, lost, all the wonderful promises in him gone and no matter now that this was somebody else's fault. Everything bad that happens is the fault of somebody or something.

I hate him, said Evelyn to herself, sharing her tearful fury with the dark ceiling. He's got no right to do this to Buell and me. Or to Reba. Or to Mama and Dad and Theo. When they catch him and put him in jail I'm not going to go see him or even write to him. I hope they put him in a hole with rats and roaches and he won't ever get to see or hear a bird again.

The little animal on the roof was back and at his scratching again, and Evelyn rose up to lean and plant a fierce kiss on the back of Buell's neck. Whispering in his ear, she said, "Tomorrow we're going home and when we get there I'm going to be so good to you you'll think I'm an angel come to live with you. I'm going to teach you how to ride my bike. Won't that be nice?"

"Nice," sighed Buell, twitching in his dream.

"And we're both going to stop loving Camfield so much," continued Evelyn.

"All right," agreed Buell in his sleep.

The next morning he rose ahead of her, took his clothes to the bathroom to dress and then went to the kitchen. Before she went to the kitchen she packed all of the clothes they had brought with them and then checked her money supply. After what their two bus tickets would cost there would be only fourteen cents left over, but the trip home was only a matter of a little over three hours. Three hours on an empty stomach never killed anybody.

Standing at the sink in the bathroom, Evelyn brushed her teeth twice and steeled herself for an argument with Buell. He would, she knew, start screaming the minute she picked up the phone, first to phone Reba and then the bus station and then the grandparents. Buell might have to be dragged from the house and down the road to the gate and she might have to wrestle him to the ground and sit on him till the bus came. The driver and his passengers might think he was being kidnapped. In words Buell never lied, but his shy, somber silences were a gift and, when he turned them on as he did sometimes when cornered or caught in a pinch, they worked for him better than a thousand words.

The kitchen was sun-filled and Buell was at the table swigging whitened coffee. A place had been laid for Evelyn and covered with a large napkin. She sat before it but did not immediately lift the square of soft white paper to see what it concealed.

Neat and neatly mannered, Buell said, "Camfield's already gone to work. He said we could go out and look around if we wanted to, but to stay away from the corrals. He said Henry might be home and we could go see him if we wanted to. You want to?"

"John Brown's mother said that coffee wasn't good for growing boys and girls," said Evelyn, coddling herself, putting off the task of going to the phone. It was black and sat on a stand beside the refrigerator. "At home," said Evelyn, "I'll bet Grandma and Grandpa are lonesome for us. They're old and what if one of them was to fall off the roof and break something while we're down here having a good time? Then we'd be sorry."

"Who's John Brown's mother?" asked Buell.

"I don't know," said Evelyn. "Some lady who

didn't want her children to drink coffee. She was in a song and we used to sing it at school. I had the best dream last night."

"Mine was funny," said Buell, sipping his milk-coffee.

"I dreamed we were home and I gave you my bicycle. First I taught you how to ride it. If I give it to you you'll have to learn how to ride it. It's not hard. You won't have any trouble because you've got nice long legs."

"Yes, they're nice and long," said Buell, collector of rocks, family snapshots and old doorknobs. He crossed and uncrossed his short legs. "Aren't you going to eat?"

"I've got to make some phone calls," said Evelyn. She lifted the napkin from her plate and was dealt a cut that went through and through her. There on the otherwise bare, cheap dish lay a long-stemmed flower, all cream-white perfection spangled with pollen dust, a bit of the wild, an expression of good, a message, a collision.

Claimed by this sight, conquered and trapped by it, Evelyn drew back and out of a full and ragged heart said, "Oh."

"It's a present from Cam," said Buell.

"I know that. Don't you think I know that?"

"He had to go a long way after it and then come back. He thought you'd like it."

"I do, Buell. I do."

"Then why are you mad at it? It's not its fault it's not bigger."

"I'm not mad at it, you little yahoo. You don't understand anything. You don't know anything."

"I know I'm not a yahoo," said Buell. "You going to phone?"

"Phone? Phone who?"

"You said you had to phone somebody."

"You're a yahoo," raved Evelyn. "You don't know anything and you don't understand anything. I can't phone now. There's nobody to phone. They wouldn't understand any more than you do. Pass me the salt."

"What're you going to put it on?" asked Buell.

"My eggs," said Evelyn.

"But they aren't cooked yet," reasoned Buell. "They're still in the refrigerator. Hey, you aren't supposed to eat that!"

"Buell," said Evelyn with her mouth full of flower, "I can't phone anybody. I can't ask anybody. We have to stay because I have to help, only I don't know how."

"If you want to know anything," advised Buell, "you should ask Cam. He knows how to do everything and he'll tell you. He's very smart and he's so good. I made his bed so when he comes home he won't have to do it."

"While I eat you'd better go make ours," said Evelyn, springing up. After she had cooked her eggs she found that she had no appetite for anything solid and downed a cup of warm, sweetened coffee, rinsed the cup, and restored it to its cupboard before Buell came back to the kitchen. He wanted to know why their clothes were packed and she said, "I did it while I was thinking about something else. We'll go see Henry if you want."

The sun was up and full, and in a closed pasture not far removed from the road curving around Camfield's house a man rode a machine that appeared to have an appetite for earth and weeds. Major Peacock's Jeep was parked in the center of the field and he and Henry Workman were leaned against one of its fenders watching the metal monster.

"What is it?" asked Buell.

"It's an eat-and-spit machine," replied Evelyn. "Don't talk so loud. Let's just inch on by. I don't want Major Peacock to see us. There's a creek out here somewhere. Let's go see if we can find it."

"An eat-and-spit machine!" cried Buell. "Oh, I want to see what it does." He gave a couple of kangaroo jumps, left the road, streaked to the fence, threw himself to the ground, and rolled under the fence's lowest, barbed strand. Then he was on his feet in the pasture and running toward Major Peacock and Henry. They saw him, and Henry pushed himself away from the Jeep and started toward him.

"Buell!" roared Evelyn, running to the fence. "I told you you were a yahoo! Now do you believe me?

You're not supposed to be in there. Get on back here with me! Buell!"

The machine had traveled down to the far end of the field, was turning, stopping, backing. Its operator left it, walked a few steps away from it, bent to examine something on the ground. The Major was paying no attention to Evelyn or Buell or Henry. Still lounged against the fender of the Jeep, he was watching the machine as if he might, even from his position, detect some flaw, an error, something unnecessary in it. When it stopped he moved to the driver's side of the Jeep, leaned in and sounded its horn three times. By this time Henry had Buell by the hand and was bending to him as an older person does when reasoning with a child.

Still at the fence, Evelyn wondered what the Major would say when he saw her without her puncher hat and boots and wondered which would be easier, to go over the fence or crawl under it. She decided to crawl under it and a moment later stood in the field. Its sod-heads quivered in the wind and the light on it was sure and clear. Evelyn started out across it, intending to snatch Buell from Henry and haul him back to the road. A muscle in her knee jerked and under her hair her scalp was damp. The muscle in her knee continued to jerk and she stopped to give it a rest.

At the far end of the pasture something was happening. Astride Spirit, Camfield had appeared and Evelyn watched him leave the animal's back and go over the fence. The machine operator was standing with one foot raised, and as Camfield reached him and took hold of him he lowered his foot and pointed. Camfield yelled but what he yelled Evelyn did not hear.

Within several yards of her Buell and Henry both swung around. Henry dropped Buell's hand and started running toward the Jeep. Major Peacock was already in it and was again sounding its horn.

"What's the matter?" shrilled Buell, steaming up to Evelyn. "What happened? What're they doing? Let's go see. Can we go see?"

"No, no, and no!" grated Evelyn. "And don't run away from me again unless you want me to cancel you. Pull up your pants. And wipe your face. No, not on my shirt. Use your own. Let's sit down on this nice clean grass and wait. Pretty soon somebody will come and tell us what happened."

So they sat on dusty clumps of grass and waited and watched. The Jeep, with both Major Peacock and Henry in it, spun away to the far end of the field and there was a flurry of activity involving first the machine operator and then the fence. A dismantled section of it lay, shortly, on the ground and the Jeep, being driven by Camfield, went over it and onto the road. The machine operator sat beside him, sat erect. As the vehicle thundered past Evelyn and Buell they saw the man's face, strangely composed. The windows to the Jeep were down and Camfield slowed long enough to yell, "Go back to the house! Get out of that field! Snakes!"

"See," said Evelyn. "I told you all we had to do

was wait here to find out what happened. That man was bitten by a snake and now Cam has to take him to a doctor."

"Is he going to die?" asked Buell.

"Of course not," said Evelyn. "The doctor will just squeeze the poison out and give him a little old squirt of medicine and then Cam will bring him on back." Abruptly aware of the impact of living, of health and whole-being, and conscious of a sudden of what the opposite of living was, she controlled a shudder. Once while on a vacation tour with her parents she had stood before a cage and watched a pit viper, a rattlesnake, restlessly coil and uncoil himself. Then she had felt nothing for the creature but now, remembering his flat, ugly head and the rage in his lidless eyes, she experienced a twinge of stern sorrow. "Snakes," she said, "live everywhere, not just here. What you have to do when you see one is run. Don't try to poke him or get down and see what he looks like. Run. That's what I do. Some snakes are dangerous. Velda Grace Renfroe has a gold bracelet shaped like one and it turns her arm green. See what I mean?"

Buell said yes, he saw what she meant. Back at the house they looked around for things to do to take their minds off snakes. Until the Major arrived they sprawled on the floor in front of the television set which produced a black and white picture of a man showing his audience how to grow big muscles.

The Major asked for a glass of iced water and sat at the table in the kitchen while he drank it. For Buell he had a weak, tolerant smile and for Evelyn a strong, shiny one. He asked her why she wasn't wearing her new boots and hat.

"I'm saving them," said Evelyn, "so when I go home they'll still be new. What about the man who was snake bitten?"

The Major looked at her as if she had called upon him to explain the floor or the garbage pail. "Why, he was snake bitten. It was his own fault. It needn't have happened. After he ran over the first one he should have stayed on his machine, but no, he had to get down and look. He's a loser and I should've known better than to hire him. A fella like him who's been around this country all his life should know about snakes. He ought to have known they like to hide in gopher holes."

"Snakes are everywhere," said Buell, excusing their existence. "Not just here. And when you see one you should run. That's what I'm going to do."

The Major pushed his glass aside and rose. "Yes. Well, what I'm going to do is get on about my business. I'm a man short now and it's going to cost me in time not to mention money. When Cracker gets back tell him I said for him to get on out there and finish up that field. But tell him I said to bring my Jeep up to the house first."

The Major was adept at mounting his borrowed horse yet, on Spirit's back, riding away from Camfield's house, there was no skill in the way he sat forward in the saddle and jerked on Spirit's reins. To

Evelyn he appeared smaller than his usual size. She and Buell went back to the television and ate ice cubes sprinkled with salt while waiting for Camfield. When he came he said that the snakebite victim had been given emergency treatment at the hospital and would be there awhile. "He's plenty sick," said Camfield, "and one of the meanest parts of this whole thing is there's no one to notify. He has no family and hasn't been here long enough to make any friends."

"He shouldn't have got down from his machine to look at the snake he ran over," said Buell with his face averted.

"He shouldn't have been wearing ordinary shoes," said Cam. "He should have been wearing boots, if not the snakeproof kind then at least the ordinary kind like these I have on. If I were in charge here I'd insist on all the men wearing them. They're expensive but they do offer some protection and so they're worth every dollar."

"Boots," said Evelyn. "Are you telling us that we have to wear boots now when we go out?"

"And loose, long-legged pants," said Camfield. "Those tight skinny ones like Buell has on now are not much more protection than his skin."

"They're the only kind he has and he doesn't have any boots," said Evelyn.

"And thick socks," said Camfield. "Both of you wear thick socks."

"Thick socks," said Evelyn. "You want me to stuff my feet into thick socks and wear boots too? Well,

I can't do it. There won't be any room left over for my feet."

"Yes there will," said Camfield. "You're just looking around now for an excuse. Let me tell you something about snakes. They're creatures to be respected. They'll let you go your way if you let them go theirs. The rule is, don't go poking into their hiding places. They like their old stumps and trash piles and hollow trees, so steer clear of those. And wear the kind of clothing I'm telling you about. I tell you what we'll do. I'll quit work early this afternoon and we'll all go into town and get the things both of you need for tramping around in the woods and fields. And then we'll have our dinner at The Orange Blossom Cafe. Mr. Jim's dinner hour is never rushed and after we eat you can stay with Reba and visit while I go over to the hospital to check on our man. I've got even another idea to go along with that one. From now on we'll have our dinner every evening at Mr. Jim's."

"Boots," exulted Buell. "I'm going to have a pair of real cowboy boots."

That the boots for him were not available in Belle Plain, that they had to be telephone ordered, that until they came, the fields and woods were forbidden territories did not dampen his spirits. During the remainder of that day and for the following three days he and Evelyn spent many of their hours on the back stoop of the prairie house watching Camfield create first a pasture of pearl millet and then one of cowpeas, for it was planning time and planting time.

The cattle would need feed for the winter months ahead and what was planted now would provide some of it. In a roundup cowboys on horseback rode across the ranges driving cattle toward corrals.

During this time Evelyn lived in two worlds, one of fact and one of make-believe. Her fact world contained knowledge that was real and raw. To avoid its fear and anxiety, its despair and burden of aloneness, she drew away from it, pretending that it did not exist.

There was comfort and power in her pretend world. It took reality away. She found a dead mouse under the stoop and, holding it aloft, chased Buell around and around the house, sharing her mischievous glee with him. She wrote a newsy letter to the Grandparents Chestnut and under her signature drew a grinning face. Her conversations with Camfield and Reba were light. Four St. Louis picture postcards arrived.

The only time the phone rang was when Reba called in the mid-afternoons to chat, to tell Evelyn and Buell what they might expect for their dinner. In the yard they squatted beside a mound of earth to observe the endless toiling of an ant colony.

On Wednesday evening Camfield came from the hospital with a cheerful report. The snakebite patient had asked that his hairy face be shaved and that his smelly head be given a washcloth shampoo.

On Thursday morning at ten o'clock Reba phoned to say that the boots and other snake protection items had arrived and at eleven o'clock a crew from the electric company came. Beginning at the entranceway to the road running past Camfield's house a long line of poles topped with frosted bulbs was planted. Through squinted eyes Evelyn watched this procedure and when it was done she cleaned her God box, taking special care with its engraved lid. In the box she placed the headless and now lifeless stem of the wild flower, the one that had been a present from Cam.

Seven

AT THE WINDOWS there was the colorless sheen of yet another day already hours old and in the house, in the room, there was someone, stealthy of footstep, who didn't belong.

Evelyn turned her head on its pillow and looked up into the face of Lavaliere. Her hair and eyes and teeth shone. She was eating a banana.

"I didn't hear you knock," said Evelyn.

"I didn't," said Lavaliere. "If you want your door knocked on you should get up and latch it when everybody else leaves. Do you know what time it is?"

"I didn't hear the rooster crow," said Evelyn.

"It's almost twelve o'clock and I've already been down and swilled all the hogs twice and put out the family wash."

"I'll bet," said Evelyn.

Lavaliere finished the banana and as she dangled its skin from her pretty fingers asked, "What do you want me to do with this?"

"Why don't you throw it under the bed?" said Evelyn. "That's what I do with everything I'm through with."

Lavaliere folded the banana skin, daintily stored it in the pocket of her skirt, went to a corner and sat on the floor. "The Major is sick."

"Sick in particular or sick in general?" asked Evelyn.

"He's got a cold," answered Lavaliere, unconcerned. And said, "It's all right if you shed those pajamas and get dressed in front of me. I won't look if you don't want me to. The Major wants to see you. I've got his Jeep outside and Cam said for me to tell you it would be all right if you went up to see what he wanted and then go on to town with me. He said if you do go to town with me to wait for him at Mr. Jim's cafe. He and Buell will be there around six-thirty or seven o'clock."

Naked, Evelyn crossed the room to her suitcase, pawed its rumpled contents and selected white underwear, heavy green socks, black jeans with flared legs and a dark blue, long-sleeved shirt. "I didn't hear Cam leave the house. Where did you see him?"

"He and some of the Major's other shoe leather cowboys are dipping cattle today," said Lavaliere, admiring her sleek legs. "He's got Buell with him. You ever seen cattle being dipped?"

"No," said Evelyn, "and I don't want to either."

"It doesn't hurt them. They like it. Gets rid of their ticks and lice. I've never seen one drown in a vat. Cattle can swim. Maybe you didn't know that."

"If I had ticks and lice on me I wouldn't want anybody to make me swim around in a tub filled with medicine," said Evelyn, sitting on the edge of the bed to pull on her socks and boots. "I'd just pick them off. Colds are catching," she said. "And if the Major's got one I don't want him to give it to me. I've got enough germs in me already."

"When the Major has a cold he wears a mask," said Lavaliere.

"A what?"

"A doctor's mask. It hooks over his ears and covers up his nose and mouth."

"The Major's only got one ear," observed Evelyn.

"He manages," said Lavaliere.

"Are you going to feed me when we get to the Major's house?" asked Evelyn. "Where's that silly hat he bought me?"

"It's on your head," said Lavaliere.

She drove the Jeep away from Camfield's house and across the Major's sun-bound kingdom with fire in her eyes. In the hammocks there was tucked shade.

"Where did you learn to drive?" asked Evelyn.

"I taught myself when I was ten years old," answered Lavaliere. "We had a piece of a car then." Abandoning the road, she cut across two seared fields and brought the Jeep to a stop beside the fenced lot where Major Peacock kept his show calf. The animal was in his dim, roomy stall, which had burlap tacked over its window openings, and with rake and shovel Henry Workman was cleaning the lot, managing the job of this with the stump of his arm and his one normal hand as if this work was a proud privilege.

He told Evelyn that the calf he was fitting out to be a show animal was not encouraged to loaf in the hot sun. "But I come down here of a morning every morning before the sun gets a good start and rinse him and brush him and clean his stall and feed him his grain. I have to feed him two or three times a day and in the evenings, soon as it cools off, he has to have his exercise. He keeps me on the hop but you just wait. Come show time he's the one that's going to hold the judge's eye. The Major wants a winner this year and I've promised him he'd get one." Henry's shirt was stained to the waist with his sweat. The pen was his garden and the animal who lived in it was his noble responsibility. With every pull of his rake and every hoist of his shovel he grunted his breath, yet he continued his awkward, lopsided toil.

Evelyn watched Henry's feet in their repaired shoes and said to Lavaliere, "That's your father."

"Yes," said Lavaliere.

"So why don't you get in there and help him get that mess done? You're bigger than he is and you've got two hands."

Tender of smile and sweet of eye, Lavaliere gave her reply. "Because it would hurt him if I did. He needs to work and too much of it has been taken away from him already." Watching her father pause and lean against the handle of his rake, she called out to him, "Daddy, the Major is sick so I've got to go to town for him in a little bit. I've got a list of things a mile long to see about for him and a little something to do for myself too, so it'll probably be dark before I get back."

Wet and dirty and frowning his concern, Henry

dropped his rake and came to the fence. "The Major's sick? He was down here with me early this morning and asked me to have supper with him this evening. I thought he looked a little peaked, but he didn't say anything about being sick. What's the matter with him?"

"It's just a little cold," said Lavaliere without indifference, without sympathy.

"And what's he doing for it?" worried Henry.

"He's taking pills," answered Lavaliere, "but he's just about out of them. That's one of the reasons I have to go to town. Do you need anything?"

"No," said Henry, "I got everything I need. Look at my pupil. I think he's mad at me. He likes sleeping out here in the grass but he's been eating so much of it that he's skimping on his grain feed, so today I'm going to cut it close and see if that don't clear up the problem." In the center of the lot again, Henry made Evelyn think of a little metal man Buell owned. Because of much handling and some abuse much of its bright paint was gone and one of its arms flopped, yet when wound with its key it still was able to goose step, marching to a tune no one had ever heard. Evelyn did not doubt that Henry also carried an inner tune around with him. Anybody who would shoot his own hand off to save a friend from the jaws of an alligator couldn't be tuneless. The Major was the tuneless one. Probably he had spent his part of the war in the South Pacific hounding alligators and stuffing dead buzzards to make them look real again.

In the Jeep again, Evelyn started working up a case against the Major and when, forty-five minutes later, she entered the living room where he sat waiting for her, she was ready for him. The food she had eaten in his kitchen made her feel strong and independent and scrappy.

Major Peacock was in a scrappy mood himself. He was not wearing the promised doctor's mask and said, "You took your time about getting here, didn't you?"

"I didn't know you had bought my time," said Evelyn. "Where's that mask Lavaliere said you'd be wearing?"

"I can't breathe through it," said the Major. "Sit down and tell me what you think."

"About what?"

"Anything. The story of your life if you can't think of anything else."

"Well," said Evelyn, "I was born twelve years ago but you don't want to hear the rest."

"Why don't I?"

"Because I haven't done anything since."

"You aren't supposed to have done anything," declared the Major peevishly. "You're just a kid and all you're supposed to do is have a good time so when you get old like I am now you'll have some good times to remember. What'd you do yesterday?"

"Fooled around. Watched a movie on television. We're only supposed to watch certain kinds unless we have special permission, but there wasn't anybody to ask so we did anyway. The movie scared Buell and I didn't like it. All about people in jail. After that I wrote a letter to my mom and dad, and last evening we went to town with Camfield and had our dinner at The Orange Blossom Cafe and then we went to the hospital."

"The hospital? What for?"

"To see the man the snake bit."

"Oh, him," said Major Peacock. "How is he?"

"Sick," said Evelyn. "But he isn't going to die."

"Well, that's one load off my mind," said the Major. "If he had died I just know I would have been stuck with his funeral bill, part of it anyway."

For one awful and empty moment Evelyn felt herself in darkness, cut off from everything she knew to be just and decent. The Major's face remained attached to his neck and his neck remained on the back of his lounge chair, but there was something wrong with his face, the way it narrowed and shrunk until it was no more. But then its mouth reappeared and the voice issuing from it, repeating, said, "I say I like you in that hat. Lavaliere's fixing to go to town for me and I'd like you to go with her and stop by my store and pick up the rest of your stuff."

Said Evelyn, "What rest? I don't have any stuff at your store."

The Major wheezed his happy generosity. "You have too. I phoned Reba and she helped me out with the sizes and I ordered it and it all came this morning, two outfits."

"The man in the hospital," said Evelyn. "He's worried about his job. When we go see him tonight can I tell him he can come back to work for you when he gets out?"

The Major studied the little jar in his hand, unscrewed its lid and began smearing his temples and his upper lip with its medicated salve. "Kid, I got me this cold and can't be worrying about that man in the hospital. You said he wasn't going to die and he's going to come out of there with all of his bills paid. Now if you ask me, or even if you don't, it looks to me like that would be enough for anybody. What's it to you whether that mossback comes back to work for me or not? He's not your problem."

"He's got no family and he hasn't been here long enough to make any friends," said Evelyn. Horrified, she felt her eyes mist and her nose redden. "But I guess you're right," she said. "I guess he's not my problem."

The Major scooped a gob of the salve from its jar and plopped it into his mouth.

"I guess he's not anybody's," said Evelyn.

The Major began to look around as if he might see a reward for being himself come from one of the walls. "I put in the lights for you and they cost me more then I had figured on spending."

"They're nice," said Evelyn. "Last night after we got home we put up dark shades on all the windows to Camfield's house so the lights won't keep anybody awake when they're trying to sleep, and then I went for a walk by myself. The lights are nice. Thank you."

"My money don't grow in fish ponds," argued Major Peacock, picking up some spirit. "When I tell a man to do a job and I'm paying him to do it I want it done. I don't like having to pay two men to do one job."

"It wasn't his fault the snake bit him," said Evelyn.

"It wasn't mine either," said the Major.

"It was on your property."

"By accident. I didn't invite it."

"I said that man wasn't anybody's problem," flashed Evelyn. "He's not mine and he's not yours so why don't we quit talking about him?"

"Because I've got the feeling we aren't going to be finished with him till I say I'll take him back when he gets out of the hospital," said Major Peacock. "There might be a law that maybe will try to force me into it, but I don't force so easy. If I don't take him back, is that going to finish things between you and me?"

"They might not be the same," said Evelyn. Her eyes had cleared and her nose had cooled.

The Major plopped another gob of the salve into his mouth, rolled it around on his tongue and swallowed it. Sorrowfully stubborn, he said, "Well, Kid, in that case it'll have to be quits for you and me. I can't have you telling me how to run my business. On your way out tell Lavaliere I said Henry is coming to eat supper with me so she should leave enough cold stuff in the refrigerator for two. Oh, and if you go on to town with her don't bother stopping by my store. There won't be anything there for you."

Commanded, dismissed, Evelyn left her chair and the Major. She had failed the man in the hospital, yet within her there was a sense of relief and increase as though something in her head had widened and broadened. She felt that she had been someplace and had climbed a height where the air was cleaner and sharper, where there was no clutter and no need to create any.

Dressed for the trip to town and waiting for her in the kitchen, Lavaliere was checking the refrigerator shelves. "I already know Daddy's coming for supper with the Major and it's all in there waiting for them except the coffee, and I guess one of them can manage that." She slammed the refrigerator door. "I got me a swell new fella. He works for the electric company and goes to night school so he can get to be an engineer, but he's going to meet me at seven and we're going to have us a little hour date. What's funny?"

"Nothing," answered Evelyn, grinning. In the Jeep she took the cowgirl hat from her head and slung it onto the backseat and all the way into Belle Plain, while Lavaliere gabbled away at the subject of her new boyfriend, sat with her elbows propped on her knees and her face in her hands staring out at the flat, sun-scorched land, blue-hazed where the trees knotted and green around the waterholes and the creek and wet ponds.

Today, in this hour, she was at a truce with the prairie and the claims it had made on her. A part of her, the part that had sought the answers to Camfield and for him, had disappeared. She had come to a truce with herself as well, for was she not just a kid? Yeah. A big one but still only a kid, barely able to judge her own actions and mistakes, let alone those of others. It was as if she had been to a doctor and he had said to her, "Now I'm not going to tell you why you've been hurting because you wouldn't understand. You don't need to understand. Go home. Take these pills every four hours and don't worry. Let me do the worrying. I'm the specialist."

It was like that. And now, on her way to Belle Plain with Lavaliere, Evelyn rolled down the window on her side of the Jeep and sucked hot, sweet air into her lungs. How good it was to be only twelve.

In Mr. Jim's cafe she sat at the end of the counter and ate a sample of Greek-style eggplant. The cafe's front window awnings had been lowered against the afternoon sun. The place was empty of customers. In his kitchen Mr. Jim and his cashier discussed public health rules and the price of cabbage. Reba stood in back of the counter folding cloth napkins.

"Some job you've got here," commented Evelyn. "You really like it?"

"I like it," said Reba. "Mr. Jim is nice to me. Nice to Cam too. And the money I'm making and saving, that's nice too."

"Camfield and Buell will be here about six-thirty or seven o'clock."

"You told me."

"What are you going to do with the money you're saving?"

Reba's look was far away and busy. It was a woman's look and a wife's. "Buy some things for the place Cam and I are going to have when we leave here and go someplace else."

"Is Cam really going to be a farmer?"

"I don't know. He keeps telling me that's what he wants to do."

"Does getting to be a farmer cost a lot of money?"

"I suppose it does," answered Reba, attacking a fresh stack of unfolded napkins. "Right now I'm not thinking about that part of it. I'm letting Camfield do all the thinking. He says he's got it all figured out how we're going to manage."

Evelyn made her counter stool swivel. "The eggplant was good. I think I'll have some more for my dinner tonight. May I go over to your room for a little while? I'm dirty and want to wash."

"You may go," said Reba, "but if you want to wash you'll have to use one of the upstairs' bathrooms. The sink in my room is out of whack. The plumber was supposed to have fixed it yesterday but only made it worse. This evening when Cam comes he'll go over and take care of it."

So this was how the matters of Evelyn and those who belonged to her stood at mid-afternoon on this day. Walking to Reba's rooming house, she saw that the town's playground was alive with supervised children who splashed and laughed and fought and bled and were consoled and laughed again. The keepers of Belle Plain's businesses were at their affairs. From a window one smiled at Evelyn and she smiled back. The day was not perfect but it was worth a smile, worth following.

Eight

THERE WAS A SAMENESS about the dinner hour at The Orange Blossom Cafe. Experiencing it for the fifth time Evelyn observed the outside window awnings being raised at a precise time, watched Reba going from table to table checking the napery and place settings, saw the cashier come to take up her position at the cash register, heard Mr. Jim say, "Going to be a slow night." His high chef's hat and cook's apron were dazzling white and in his kitchen there was radio music.

Evelyn, Buell and Camfield ate their dinner at one of the back tables and when they had finished, Camfield borrowed an assortment of tools from Mr. Jim and left. He said he didn't know how long it would take him to fix the ailing sink in Reba's room.

Evelyn said, "We'll wait." The small rabbity man hunched over his newspaper at the counter and two young women, paired off at one of the front tables, had taken her interest on Monday night, but now there was nothing more of them to analyze, to question. The man's face was shaped like one of those long baking potatoes from Idaho and she decided that both of the women hungered for something other than food, but were afraid to go out and look for it.

The three diners took Buell's interest. To quiet

him, to satisfy his fidgety curiosity, Evelyn invented backgrounds for them. "The man is from Idaho," she said. "He used to be a potato grower."

"Where's Idaho?" asked Buell.

"It's out West. Where potatoes and those white beans Grandma makes soup out of come from. Eat your pudding. You want me to eat it for you?"

"No," said Buell. "I can do it. What about those ladies?"

"The one with the red hair works in a bank."

"Did she tell you that?"

"No, but I can tell. She's got green eyes. They used to be brown but now because she has to look at green money all day long they're green. I can't say what her name is."

"What about the other one?"

"She used to live in a lighthouse and help her father rescue the struggling seamen when their ships would run into each other. Now she's a violin teacher."

"Did she tell you that?"

"No, but I know it because I'm good at figuring people out."

Buell dipped his spoon into his pudding, fished the cherry from its vanilla depths and popped it into his mouth. "I don't like having to wait for somebody. Let's go over to Reba's room and help Camfield fix her sink."

"We'd be in his way," reasoned Evelyn. "Eat your pudding and think nice thoughts. That always makes the time go faster when you're waiting for somebody."

"Nice thoughts," said Buell and set his eyes on the wall clock. Its electric hands stood at ten minutes past eight when Camfield returned to the cafe scouting for yet more tools. After one look at his strained face Buell ducked his head, concealing his own weariness. Alone and encouraged by some brief instruction from Mr. Jim, Camfield went back to Reba's room.

At eight-thirty, two quartets of late diners and coffee drinkers arrived and immediately after them Lavaliere blew in. Fresh from her stolen time with the night-student engineer, and heavily scented with a perfume that made Evelyn wince, she was wreathed in rosiness and full of talk and hurry. To Evelyn and Buell she said, "I was going by and just happened to look in and spotted you two sitting back here, but I didn't see Cam's truck so I went around the block again and here I am. Where's Cam?"

"He's over at Reba's room fixing her busted sink and we're sitting here thinking nice thoughts so we won't notice how long it's taking him," said Evelyn.

"Camfield is so good," sighed Buell. "He's what my nice thoughts are about."

"Cam is a lot of things," commented Lavaliere, "but a plumber isn't one of them. One time I saw him fix a sink for the Major and it took him four trips to town and six hours. I'm on my way home now. I'm running late so I'm in a hurry. You want to ride with me? It'd beat sitting around here waiting."

Drooping and bleary-eyed, Buell said, "No, we

told Cam we'd wait here." He was still protesting when Mr. Jim lifted him from his chair and carried him out to the Major's Jeep. The streets of Belle Plain were artificially lighted.

Out on the country road, the one leading away from town, there was a different kind of light, high aloft. The moon was up and under its giant orange sail the prairie rested. So lighted was the landscape that it was possible, from the moving car, to identify shapes and forms; bare stretches of white sands, oak and palm hammocks, old stumps, the skeleton of a once-occupied wayside house. There were miles of free, open country and running parallel to the road there were deep dry ditches and above these there was higher, grassed land.

Fully awake now and in good humor again, Buell sat in the back seat of the Jeep with his nose pressed against the window. He wanted to know what made the moon and Evelyn said, "It's the moon like this is the earth, and like we're people."

"What if it was to fall down on us?" asked Buell.

"It's not going to fall down on us," replied Evelyn. "It's stuck up there good. Don't worry about it."

"Is it hot or cold?"

"Cold," said Evelyn. She had fastened herself into her seat with its safety belt and shoulder harness, and so when Lavaliere brought the Jeep to a sudden, squealing stop only her neck felt the jolt. The road ahead was straight and flat and now, standing guard over field and pasture, there were the well-tended fences of the Peacock ranch.

"What's wrong?" asked Buell. "What are we stopping here for? Did you run over something?"

"The Major's cold pills," said Lavaliere, flustered. "I forgot them. We'll have to go back for them."

"Clear back to town?" said Evelyn. "You're going clear back to town for some little old cold pills? But that's crazy. I tell you what. When I get a cold all Mama does is rub me with some camphorated oil and then she ties a wool sock around my neck and I get better."

"You aren't the Major," said Lavaliere. "He wants those pills and I'll have to go back for them."

"Well," said Evelyn, "if you think you have to do it then you have to do it, but not Buell and me. We'll get out and walk the rest of the way."

"It's at least a mile and a half to Cam's gate," cautioned Lavaliere. "And I don't know about leaving you out here on the road by yourself."

Evelyn got out of the car, opened its back door and pulled Buell from it. She did not want to walk. What she wanted was to get away from Lavaliere's perfume. She wanted the purity of the country air and she wanted bed and the comfort of sleep. "A mile and a half is nothing," she said. "One time Buell and I walked up a whole mountain all by ourselves. At night. In the dark. Didn't we, Buell?"

"Yes," said Buell, "but I don't remember it."

"Naturally," said Evelyn. "You were only four then. Come on. We won't walk in the road. There's no water in the ditch and if we go on over to the other side of it we'll be able to see some interesting things. It's higher over there."

Buell watched Lavaliere drive away and, following Evelyn down through the ditch and up onto the high ground on its opposite side, talked about the mountain he had never climbed. "How big was it?"

"Big," said Evelyn.

"Why did we climb it?"

"To see what was on it."

"At night?"

"It wasn't black-dark. It was brown-dark."

"What was on it?"

"A whole bunch of stuff."

"People?"

"One."

"What was he doing?"

"It was a woman."

"What was she doing?"

"Making an Easter basket."

"How many kids did she have?"

"None."

"Then who was the Easter basket for?"

"Listen," said Evelyn. "Do you remember how old you were when Grandma taught you how to swim?"

"Four," said Buell.

"So how come if you can remember that, you can't remember we never climbed a mountain when you were four?"

Ahead of her, stepping high and wide, Buell grunted. By star and by moon the empty spaces all around lay in calm.

A moving shape, a truck, had appeared in the empty road. Moving without lights, it came with a stealthy pant and, when it was almost opposite to the spot where Evelyn and Buell were, it turned in and rolled to the fence on the other side of the road.

"It's Cam!" exclaimed Buell, and ran toward the ditch. But when he got to its edge he pulled up short, wheeled and came bounding back. "No, that's not Cam. It's somebody else. Two. One's a girl. Who are they? What are they doing?"

"Be quiet," said Evelyn. "I don't know who they are or what they're doing. They're just turning around because they were going the wrong way." Her heart had begun to cough as if someone or something had reached into her and struck it. With monstrous patience she said, "Let's go back in there where those big weeds are and sit down for a minute. We don't need to watch somebody turn a truck around."

"They're taking the fence down," said Buell, his excitement and indignation rising. "They're not supposed to do that. It belongs to the Major and the cows will get out. Evvie?"

"The cows don't belong to us and the fence doesn't either and so we don't care about any of it,"

136

said Evelyn. With a startling strength, one that she didn't know she possessed, she yanked Buell to her, lifted him, staggered a half dozen steps through short, rough weeds. The stand of tall ones met her and she set her squirming burden down with a thump. Her knees and arm hinges were jerking and she fell to the ground herself and lay there looking up at Buell with a cruel glitter in her eyes. "Ah," she said. "Ah."

The pretense was over. Buell knew what was taking place in the field on the other side of the road. She saw that he did. "Don't look," she said, "and then if somebody asks, you won't have to tell what you saw. Lie down here beside sister until it's over and then we can go on to Camfield's house."

"No," said Buell, emphatically and vengefully. "I'm going to watch so when Camfield comes I can tell him what I saw and he'll know what to do." Standing, peering through the weeds, whispering, he said, "Look. Now they've got the fence down and they're taking the truck in to where the cows are. They've got their lights on. The cows are coming. Evvie, the cows are coming! The little ones! Evvie!"

"Tomorrow," murmured Evelyn weakly. "We're going home. We'll stay with Grandma and Grandpa until Mama and Dad and Theo get back from St. Louis."

"The man," hissed Buell. "He's shooting the cows. Hear it?"

"No, I don't hear anything."

"He's killing them!"

"No, he isn't. He's just putting them to sleep for a while."

"They're falling down. The calves are all falling down and the man and girl are putting them in the truck."

Spent and hideously defeated, sick with defeat, Evelyn tried imagining that she was in some kind of seal, one of those plastic refrigerator bags in which foods are stored. There was no escape in this fantasy. She could place herself in the bag but could not close it.

Still at his detective post Buell was counting. "One. Two. Three. Four. Five. Six. They've got six. That's how many they're stealing. They're all in the truck now and it's fixing to leave. The girl's getting in. She's going to drive. Now the man. He's getting in too. No, the girl can't start the truck. It won't start. Listen to it. *Grrrrr*. It won't start. Ha! Now what will they do?"

"I don't know," said Evelyn. "It doesn't matter, not to us. What matters is that they don't see us and what matters is that we don't tell Cam or anybody else about this."

Buell came to her, bent over her. "We're not even going to tell Cam? Why aren't we?"

Evelyn sat up. "Because it's part of his job to keep people from stealing the Major's cows and it would make him feel awful if he knew some had been stolen while he was in town fixing Reba's sink. And you know how he is. You know he'd go right away and tell Major Peacock and then the Major might fire him. For six cows the Major would fire Cam and he wasn't even here. Didn't you say they only got six?"

"That's how many they put in their truck," said Buell. "Six. I counted them."

"And the Major's got thousands," reasoned Evelyn. "Thousands. If you had thousands would you care about six?"

All maleness, Buell said, "It isn't Camfield's fault. He wasn't even here and didn't even see them, so he shouldn't get fired for it. Listen to them over there. *Grrrrr. Rrrrrrr.* Their crazy old truck won't start. Maybe the cows are too heavy for it. Maybe they'll have to leave them. Wouldn't that be funny? I say wouldn't that be funny?"

"Funny," agreed Evelyn, rising to her knees to part the weeds, to look out, listening not to the sounds coming from the disabled truck in the field on the other side of the road but to others. Another truck was coming, one that rattled and did not hide its lights. Down the road from Belle Plain it came and in an agony of strain and frustration and conflict Evelyn sat fastened to the ground. The approaching vehicle was a pickup and it was Camfield's.

Beside her and breathing fast, Buell said, "It's Cam. He's stopping. Evvie, he sees them and he's stopping!"

Thinking fast, inventing, Evelyn clapped a hand over Buell's mouth. "I see him. It's all right, I think it's all right. If they're stealing the cows he'll stop

139

them, but here's something I hadn't thought about. They might just be out here doing some night work. Either way we should be quiet. If I take my hand away will you do that? Will you sit here and be quiet till it's finished?"

Assenting, Buell moved his lips against her palm and she dropped it. "Night work," whispered Buell. And with her he watched Camfield descend from the pickup still parked in the road and stride toward that portion of the fence which was dismantled. Its posts, still with their fence strands attached, were lying on the ground as though they belonged there, and the man and the girl came running to the opening and met Cam in the manner of people who know each other.

"You see," said Evelyn, speaking into Buell's ear. "It's all right. I told you it was." A harsh ache ran through her. She could not put truth into her words. Helplessly she said, "It's night work. Didn't I tell you that was what it was?"

Buell drew back, turned his face from her desperate gaze. A page in his life was turning and he sat perfectly still.

Nine

So Evelyn's lies, all of them, had been for nothing, and now the only thing left to do was to sit behind the weed screen and witness truth.

At the fence opening across the road Camfield and the two rustlers held a quick conference. The girl made an angry motion, pointing to the truck loaded with the stolen calves, and Camfield went running back to his pickup, jumped into its cab and drove it into the field, placing it up close to that of the cow stealers. The man had raised its hood and now Camfield again jumped from his pickup, motor still running, went to its rear, rummaged through a box there, found what he searched for, went running back. The man had raised the hood to Cam's pickup also and now the girl was in the larger truck, seated behind its wheel, waiting.

"It was their battery that wouldn't let their truck start," offered Evelyn to the little desolated figure hunched beside her. "You remember how Grandpa used to have trouble with his car battery? And how Camfield used to always have to go and help him get his car started? I forgot the name of that thing he always used."

"Jumper cable," said Buell. "That's what Camfield told me it was." And tonelessly he said, "He's helping them steal the cows and when they get through and go I'm going too, but not back to his house. I'm not ever going back to his house. Have you got our money with you?"

"Yes."

"Enough for the bus? So we can go home tomorrow on the bus?"

"Buell," said Evelyn, "they only took six calves. And when you thought it was only the man and the girl you said you didn't care."

"I care now. When they go are you going with me?"

"Where?"

"To Belle Plain. To where Reba has her room. We can stay with her tonight."

"Buell, it's miles back to Belle Plain and Reba would want to know what was wrong. She'd ask why we had come back and what would we tell her?"

"I don't know. We wouldn't have to stay with her tonight and that way we wouldn't have to tell her anything. We could go to the bus station. Wait for the bus."

"Buell, it might not come till tomorrow morning and do you think you can walk all the way back to town?"

"I can. If you can't you can stay here, but I'm going," said Buell in the obstinate tone of one rising from a sickbed, determined to be healthy again.

A shower of hot, confused wind swept the prairie, passed over. In the field on the opposite side of the road a swift commotion was taking place. Camfield's jumper cable had done its work and now the rustler's truck, swaying a little, was moving toward the opening in the fence. The girl was at its wheel and Camfield and the other man were in Camfield's pickup, following. Both trucks moved out into the road and stopped, and all in seconds the two men were out of Cam's truck and running back into the field. Each pulled a bush from the earth and, using them as they would use brooms, swept the grass and patches of sandy ground where the truck had left marks. When they reached the fence they again established it, pulling the poles upright, setting them in their holes, pushing the grass clods back around them. Again the two brush brooms were used to erase foot and tire tracks and were then tossed into the ditch.

There was a quick last-minute inspection. Satisfied, Camfield and the man sped back to the two parked trucks. Their lights flooded the road but they did not move, for there came out of the moonlighted darkness a sleek white car. When it stopped beside the two trucks, there stepped from it a man dressed in an official uniform.

To Buell Evelyn whispered, "Don't say anything."

His finger dug into her arm and his lips moved. "Police. It's the police."

Camfield had come out of his pickup and was standing at its door. His stance was easy. The voices in the road were clear, unhurried. "What's the trouble?" the officer asked Camfield.

Camfield answered, "None now. These people were stalled here with a dead battery and I came along and gave them a hand. I always carry a jumper cable with me."

"Lucky for them," commented the officer and sauntered to the rear of the bigger truck for an investigating look. Its tailgate was up and inside its confines the animals remained quiet.

Returning to the front of the truck, the officer asked the girl and the man to step out and they obeyed instantly. "It was just a dead battery," said the man. "I reckon we'd have been here all night if this gentleman hadn't come along and helped us out. I always do that when I see somebody stuck and lost out in the end of nowhere, but most people won't do it. They just whizz right on by."

"Those calves in there," said the officer. "Where did you get them?"

"We picked them up down the road a piece," replied the cattle thief. "The wife here and I are hauling them for a man."

"I suppose you can prove that."

"Prove it?"

"Can you offer some proof as to where the calves you're hauling came from? Did the man you're hauling them for give you a paper?"

"No sir, he didn't."

"Did you ask him for one?"

"No sir, I didn't. Hauling cattle is not my regular line of work."

"What is your regular line of work?"

"Chickens. My wife and me are from Arkansas. It's big on chickens. We're on our way back there now. Florida was a mistake for us. Where we picked the calves up, it was a farm and the onliest reason we stopped there was because we were lost and it was coming on dark."

"This farm," said the officer. "What town was it near?"

"It wasn't near no town," said the rustler. "It was way out in the sticks, maybe fifty miles down the road."

"Do you think you could find it again?"

"The farm? I don't think so. My wife was asleep and I wasn't paying attention to anything except how to find my way back to the main road. That's why we stopped. We each got us a glass of water and then the man we're hauling the calves for said was we going to Belle Plain, and I told him we was going to go through it and he hired us to take the calves. The man we're going to deliver them to is going to pay us."

The trooper took a flashlight from one of his hip pockets and aimed its beam at the rustler's truck tires. "When you get to Belle Plain you'd better have those tires checked. To me the two rear ones look low on air. The man you're doing this hauling for, did he give you his name?"

The cow stealer scratched his head. "It was Joyner. No, that's the man we're supposed to deliver the calves to once we get to Belle Plain. Officer, to tell you a fact, I don't know what that farmer's name was. I was busy loading the calves and trying to understand what we were supposed to do with them once we got to Belle Plain. We're supposed to meet Mr. Joyner at the Fair Oaks Motel and he's supposed to take the calves off us and pay us. I sure hope he's not the forgetful type. This deal hasn't been nothing but trouble to me, and I'm tired of it. Tired of yesterday too. Yesterday morning when we started out, I gave my wife my wallet to hold and she put it in her purse, and when we stopped at a greasy-spoon restaurant for coffee she left it there, purse, wallet, everything. We went back for it but they said they didn't have it."

"So you don't have any personal identification either," said the officer. "Is that it?"

"Yes sir," answered the rustler. "That's about it."

Said Camfield, "I have identification. My billfold is there on the seat of my pickup if you'd care to examine it. I work for Major Peacock."

"I know you do," said the officer. He held his flashlight in his left hand and his right one rested on the butt of his holstered gun. "I've seen you around Belle Plain," he said.

The two cattle thieves were propped against the door of their truck. Whining a complaint, the girl said, "Officer, we know you're just doing your job and we appreciate it, but what are we going to do? Stand out here all night? What are you going to do? Arrest us? Take us to jail?"

Behind the weeds, crouched behind them, witnessing, Buell whispered, "Jail! He's going to take them to jail. Camfield too? Evvie? Will Camfield have to go too?"

Feebly and faintly Evelyn said, "Don't ask me. I don't know. I don't know anything." The white blur of Buell's face came at her and hung before her, but then, as though pulled by some invisible force, it moved up and back. The body supporting it parted the weeds, went through them, jogged to the ditch, plunged across it, went up its far side, tore out into the road and charged toward Camfield.

Neither the man nor the girl moved. They did not speak.

Camfield dropped to one knee, reached out to Buell, caught him, enfolded him. "Hey," he said. "Where'd you come from? Where's Evvie?"

The officer moved to stand behind Camfield. He still held his flashlight in one hand and kept his other on the butt of his gun. It was to him that Buell delivered his torrent of screams.

"She's over there and we saw it all and it was just like Cam said! All he did was help them get their truck started. He didn't steal the cows! He wasn't even here when they did it. That man and that girl over there! They're the ones! They did it. They shot the cows to make them go to sleep and then they put them in their truck and made it come back out here and then they put up the fence again and started to go away with the cows but their truck wouldn't start and that's when Cam came and helped them! He didn't do anything bad! You can't take him to jail! They're the ones who did it all!"

Still squatted among her tall, arid weeds, Evelyn's thundering heart grew quiet. Upon her ears Buell's sobbing lie fell as a rescuing line, a lifesaver's rope that pulled her from deep water to shallow, freeing her of all that had hounded and deviled her since coming to this wrong and lost place. The lie was love. It meant love and its purpose was good and right. Maybe, maybe it would jolt Camfield back from where he had been, alone and so mixed up.

The sky had changed color. Now its mighty lamp was not orange but silver and, juggling her thoughts, Evelyn rose from her huddle of weeds. From the road Camfield was calling her and his call was secure and cheerful.

So she walked to the ditch and went down into it and up its other side and stood before the others gathered in the road, and she was sure of herself, sure of her strength, sure of everything.

To the officer Camfield said, "This is Evelyn, my wife's sister." He was still kneeling, still holding Buell, stroking his hair, comforting him. "It's all right," he said. "It's all right. I'm not going to jail. Why don't you go and sit in my truck and wait for me? I won't be long."

By the officer's expression Evelyn could judge nothing. It was solemn and watchful. He kept his hand on his gun. Evelyn advanced to meet him and, respectfully, he stepped back a pace, allowing her to pass him and go to Camfield and Buell.

The man and the girl still had not moved. They also watched and waited. Evelyn looked at them only once. She felt no pity for them. They had never painted a blue prince or looked at a spinner's web. She told herself that all they knew was sin and ignorance so the world would be better off without them. They belonged in jail.

Ready to speak her own lie, Evelyn walked up to Camfield and Buell and halted. She looked down at Buell and met his upturned face and saw in it its torment and plea. And the words were in her throat but they would not come.

In silence, there came another voice, one that spun its prayerful song to the glowing night, to the heavens, to her. It came out of the wild and it was that of her bird, and though he was nowhere he was everywhere, his notes directing her, reaching into her, pointing to reality—touching all that she had been taught and learned to be truly right. The song trembled its regret and its sorrow for Camfield and sang its hope for Buell and its trust in Evelyn. Its last note spoke a reverent *Amen* and then its feathered composer fell silent.

Evelyn was crying when she spoke to Camfield. "I love you," she said. "I have always loved you, but I can't do this for you. And I can't let Buell do it for you either. Can't you see that I can't?"

Camfield put Buell away from him and stood. "Yes," he said. "Yes, of course."

The girl rustler had a spiteful comment and a question for her partner. "You should have let me do the talking. I would have said our truck was stole and we was out looking for it, and we found it in the field yonder already loaded with the calves and all we did was bring it back out here to the road. That was the story I thought we was going to tell if we was stopped and questioned. You're the one who made it up. How come you didn't remember it?"

"Because I thought my other one was better," answered the partner. "And anyway it wouldn't have differed. This time it was all stacked against us. Because of the children, it was all stacked against us."

Ten

EVELYN DID NOT SEE or hear from Major Peacock again, and her last view of the prairie was taken the next morning as she and Buell stood with Lavaliere and Reba at the gate in front of the house that had been only a sleazy and restless shelter to Camfield and Reba.

The sun was up and the prairie was at its business. The bus, Reba said, might be a few minutes late. Her soft despair did not yield to the waste of tears. It was the simple language of a young wife come now to stand by the side of a young, loved husband in trouble. Around midnight of the night just passed, she and Lavaliere had come to first sit and explain to Evelyn and Buell and then to work. The new window shades were taken down, the cupboards and drawers emptied, the packed boxes and bags carried out to Mr. Jim's car borrowed for this emergency.

Generously, Evelyn had been invited to help and once, passing Reba in the hallway, she said, "I caused all of this and if you hate me for it I won't blame you."

And Reba, holding fast and level, replied, "I don't hate you for it. You didn't cause it. You only refused to be a part of it."

"But he's in jail now," said Evelyn, fighting a wave of emotion. "And you said Mr. Jim said maybe he'll be sent to prison. For three years. Or five. He'll have to pay the same as those other two. You said so. Didn't you tell us he'd have to pay?"

"Yes," answered Reba, "but we won't know for how long or where until he goes before a judge. Please help me. Please calm down. Can't you be calm?"

"If only I hadn't heard the bird," said Evelyn.

"The bird? What bird?"

"The bird! My bird! I thought I heard him. I thought he was there. He wasn't but I thought he was!"

"Oh, honey," said Reba, guarding her composure. "Go home. Be ready when the bus comes. Take care of Buell on the way and when you get there try to be happy. Don't be sorry about any of this here. Don't worry about Cam or me. Whatever the judge decides for him, wherever he's sent, I'll be close by. Please, please stop worrying. Believe me, it won't produce a thing for you."

It was the bird, said Evelyn to herself, but did not speak of it to Reba or Lavaliere again. She left her Kissimmee Kid outfit, the boots and hat the Major had given her, on the back stoop of the wilderness house.

On the bus Buell sat beside her but spurned her companionship. His anger was savage. He refused to eat from the bag of lunch Reba had prepared.

Home. How beautiful and decent it was. Back

from St. Louis, Evelyn's father opened his piano, struck a few trial chords and winced. The piano tuner came. Evelyn's mother washed windows, shampooed carpets, and spent hours at her desk writing pages of letters to Reba and Camfield. At night the dark shapes on the lawns and in the streets did not move. They belonged there.

Buell's anger with her did not cool. She offered him her bicycle. "I don't mean only for today," she said. "It's a present. You may keep it. I'll teach you how to ride it."

"I don't want it," said Buell. "I'm never going to ride on it again and don't talk to me again either. If you do I won't listen."

So her rides through the neighborhood were solitary. The summer rains started and she pedaled through their heavy downpours, watching the houses and the tangles of clouds in the thunderwest.

Buell learned a new piano piece and one evening played it to the family gathered in the Chestnut's music room. The next day Grandpa Chestnut told Evelyn that Buell's piano skill made him shiver all over and wanted to know if it affected her in the same way.

"Yes," said Evelyn, striving for honesty. "I like his music, but there's another kind I like more."

"And what kind is that?" asked Grandpa Chestnut.

"It's out there," said Evelyn, and even as the words left her mouth she regretted them. Her grandfather was like the other members of her family. He had a quick modern mind that saw straight through to the gaps in people. He saw the gaps in her.

Said Evelyn to Grandpa Chestnut, "What I meant to say was, when I'm out riding my bike and I go by a house where somebody is playing a violin, it's like needles in me. It's peculiar because as soon as I go on by I forget it and don't think about it till next time. What are you putting that piece of tin around that pecan tree for?"

"It's a squirrel shield," said Grandpa Chestnut. "Your grandmother thinks it will outfox the little monkeys this year. It won't, but thinking is believing, I suppose."

"My school is going to have a new art teacher this year," reported Evelyn. "I thought Velda Grace Renfroe told me his last name was Maddom, but the name painted on his mailbox is Madman. Could his name really be that? Mr. Madman?"

"His name," said Grandpa Chestnut, "is Mr. Maddom. M-a-d-d-o-m. And he's not the only new one in town. There's a family named Orr and they have a boy named Donald."

"I see," said Evelyn.

"I think you don't," said Grandpa Chestnut. "But there's no rush. When you start back to school you will. Young Donald is another Wilson Padgett. You remember him?"

"Yes, I remember Wilson," replied Evelyn. "I

wish I didn't. Big freak. Big money. Big car. Big mouth. Big laugh. Big mistake."

"And Mr. Maddom is another Camfield," said Grandpa Chestnut. "Already there's been trouble between him and the Orr boy. Master Donald is the one who's been taking liberties with Mr. Maddom's mailbox. You've grown some this summer, haven't you?"

"Some," answered Evelyn.

With his hammer Grandpa Chestnut gave his handiwork a final whack. "Now," he said. "We'll find out who is the smarter, the squirrels or me. My vote goes to the squirrels."

The shield did not stop the clever, greedy squirrels. It baffled them for a day or two but after that they ignored it and ran nimbly along the overhead telephone wires, dropping into the pecan tree to examine the green nuts swelling in their husks, waiting for them to ripen.

Something good happened.

One morning Evelyn was asked to take Theo to the neighborhood park where it was cool and shady. Freshly bathed and freshly dressed, holding his play pretties, Theo sat waiting. He hummed and his smile for Evelyn contained a promise.

The park was three blocks distant from the Chestnuts' home, and during the first lap of the walk Theo leaned from his buggy and studiously dropped his toy cat.

"Well," said Evelyn, bending to straighten Theo's

155

immaculate collar, "maybe it'll be there when we come back and maybe it won't, but either way I want to tell you something, Theo. You had better watch out for me. Do you know who I used to be? The Kissimmee Kid. So now when people don't appreciate the nice things I do for them, I wait till I catch them asleep and then I cut off their toes and make wienies out of them and eat them."

Theo's eyes sought hers. He laughed and then he howled. The cat lay on the sidewalk with its long velvet tail coiled around its nose, and in a minute Evelyn went back for it. "There," she said, tucking the toy into the buggy. "There's your cat. Can you say thank you?"

"Mayjoe," said Theo, snuggling the cat and kissing its nose.

"You're so cute," said Evelyn, again pushing the buggy. "And you're so sweet to everybody else. Why can't you be sweet to me? I'm your sister."

"Thwash," said Theo, and in the middle of the next block hurled his music box from his carriage and then lay back against his pillow, waving a hand as if signaling Evelyn to stop.

She continued to plod, pushing the carriage.

"Keewart," said Theo in a voice of command.

"Keewart?" said Evelyn, making the buggy go faster. "What's keewart? Is that something I should know about?"

Theo raised himself to a sitting position and his piercing cry rent the air. "Keewart! Keewart!"

"Oh," said Evelyn, pushing faster and harder. "I see. Keewart is your music box and you want me to go back for it, don't you? Well, why don't you say so? You can say real words. You can speak English. You speak it to everybody else. I've heard you."

"Keewart," wept Theo.

Evelyn stopped the carriage, went around to its side, knelt beside it, and extended her hand to Theo, intending to try again worming her way past his distrust and dislike of her. "Theo," she said, "Theo, I'll go back for your music box in a minute, but first I want you to say a word for me. Say my name. It's not hard. You can do it. Say Evvie. Evvie. Say it. I want to hear you say it because then I'll know you know who I am and then I'll tell you some other things about me too. Things nobody else knows except Camfield."

"Thwash," said Theo, and with his tongue fished a wad of soggy food from one of his cheeks, leaned and spit it onto the back of Evelyn's hand.

"Oh, you little precious," cried Evelyn. "Wasn't that fun? Do you have any more for me? No? Well, then I guess we'll just have to get along with what we have here." With her clean hand she removed Theo's baseball cap, and as he sat without sound or motion she transfered the food mess from her soiled hand to his hair. She went back for the music box and returned it to him. "Thwash," she said and again took command of the buggy. As he had been taught to do, Theo cranked the music box and its tune tinkled.

The park was in summer color. There were bright fish and floating lilies in its formal ponds and its old magnolia trees were fiercely green. The place was empty of people.

Under one of the magnolias Evelyn drew the buggy to a stop and lifted Theo from it. "Now," she said, "we're going to sit awhile and look at all this good stuff here and try to act like we're civilized. You don't have to talk to me. All you have to do is sit. When you get hungry you may kick me and I'll give you a piece of apple or a doughnut. I brought some."

Caring for nothing, Theo sat beside her holding his music box and his toy cat. Humming, he removed his cap and picked pieces of food from his hair, sniffed them, sniffed his fingers, and then wiped them on his shirt and laughed.

"Fiend," said Evelyn. "Little fiend." The stiff leaves of the overshadowing tree rattled with some slight disturbance and she looked up, even as Theo did, and saw the bird. As though there by appointment, he stood poised, stood framed in leafage. High-crested and gleaming, he began his gleaming song.

Theo, spellbound, said, "Oh. *Whooooo*. Look. Oh."

"It's my bird," whispered Evelyn. "Yours too. Everybody's. He belongs to everybody. Hear what he's telling us? He's saying it's all right. He's telling us everything is going to be fine."

The song went on and on and Theo crept to her and crawled into her lap. He was shivering and she put her arms around him, and he said, "Evvie."

"Yes," she said. She smelled the sourness in his hair and smelled his baby sweetness and held him yet closer.